RAPUNZEL'S REVENGE

Shannon Hale
and
Dean Hale

illustrated by **Nathan Hale**

BLOOMSBURY
NEW YORK LONDON OXFORD NEW DELHI SYDNEY

Books by
Shannon Hale, Dean Hale, and Nathan Hale

RAPUNZEL'S REVENGE
CALAMITY JACK

Also by Shannon Hale

THE BOOKS OF BAYERN
THE GOOSE GIRL
ENNA BURNING
RIVER SECRETS
FOREST BORN

PRINCESS ACADEMY
PRINCESS ACADEMY: PALACE OF STONE
PRINCESS ACADEMY: THE FORGOTTEN SISTERS

BOOK OF A THOUSAND DAYS

DANGEROUS

For adults

AUSTENLAND
THE ACTOR AND THE HOUSEWIFE
MIDNIGHT IN AUSTENLAND

Also by Nathan Hale

THE DEVIL YOU KNOW
TWELVE BOTS OF CHRISTMAS
BALLOON ON THE MOON (illustrations)
ANIMAL HOUSE (illustrations)

Text copyright © 2008 by Shannon Hale and Dean Hale
Illustrations copyright © 2008 by Nathan Hale

First published in the United States of America in 2008
by Bloomsbury Children's Books
www.bloomsbury.com

Bloomsbury is a registered trademark of Bloomsbury Publishing Plc

For information about permission to reproduce selections from this book, write to
Permissions, Bloomsbury Children's Books, 1385 Broadway, New York, New York 10018
Bloomsbury books may be purchased for business or promotional use. For information on bulk
purchases please contact Macmillan Corporate and Premium Sales Department at
specialmarkets@macmillan.com

Library of Congress Cataloging-in-Publication Data
available upon request
ISBN 978-1-59990-070-4 (hardcover) • ISBN 978-1-59990-288-3 (paperback)
LCCN: 2007037670

Book design by Nathan Hale
Balloons and lettering by Melinda Hale
HushHush and Storyline fonts by Comicraft
Printed in China by RR Donnelley, Dongguan City, Guangdong
6 8 10 9 7 (hardcover)
14 16 18 20 19 17 15 (paperback)

All papers used by Bloomsbury Publishing, Inc., are natural, recyclable products
made from wood grown in well-managed forests. The manufacturing processes
conform to the environmental regulations of the country of origin.

For Christine Hale, aka Mom,
who, but for a lack of mile-long hair
and spiteful imprisonment by a witch,
could have been the hero of this story
—S. H. AND D. H.

To Lindsay, Leigh, and Layna:
three cowgirls, my sisters
—N. H.

Part 1: Once Upon a Tower

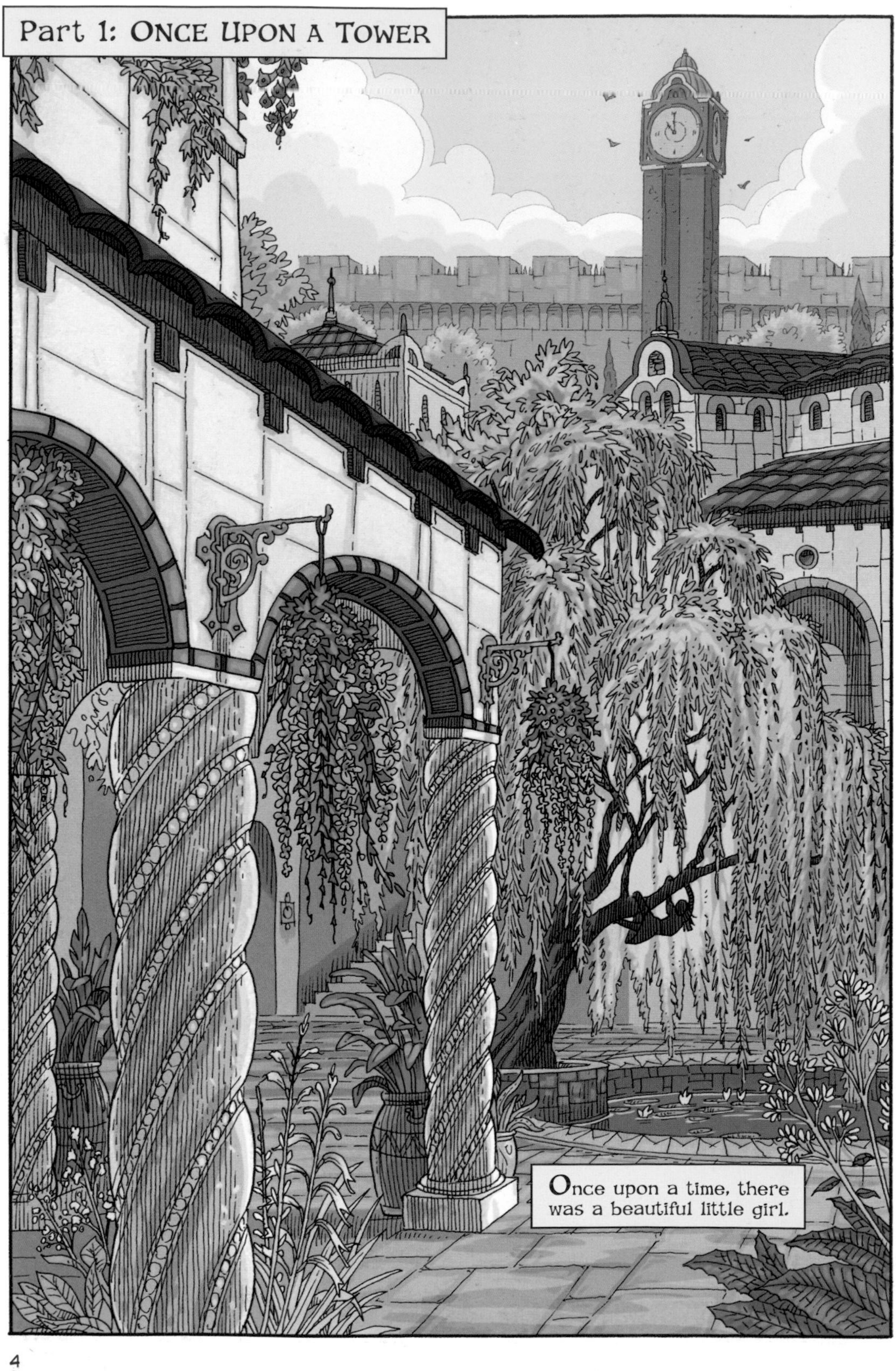
Once upon a time, there was a beautiful little girl.

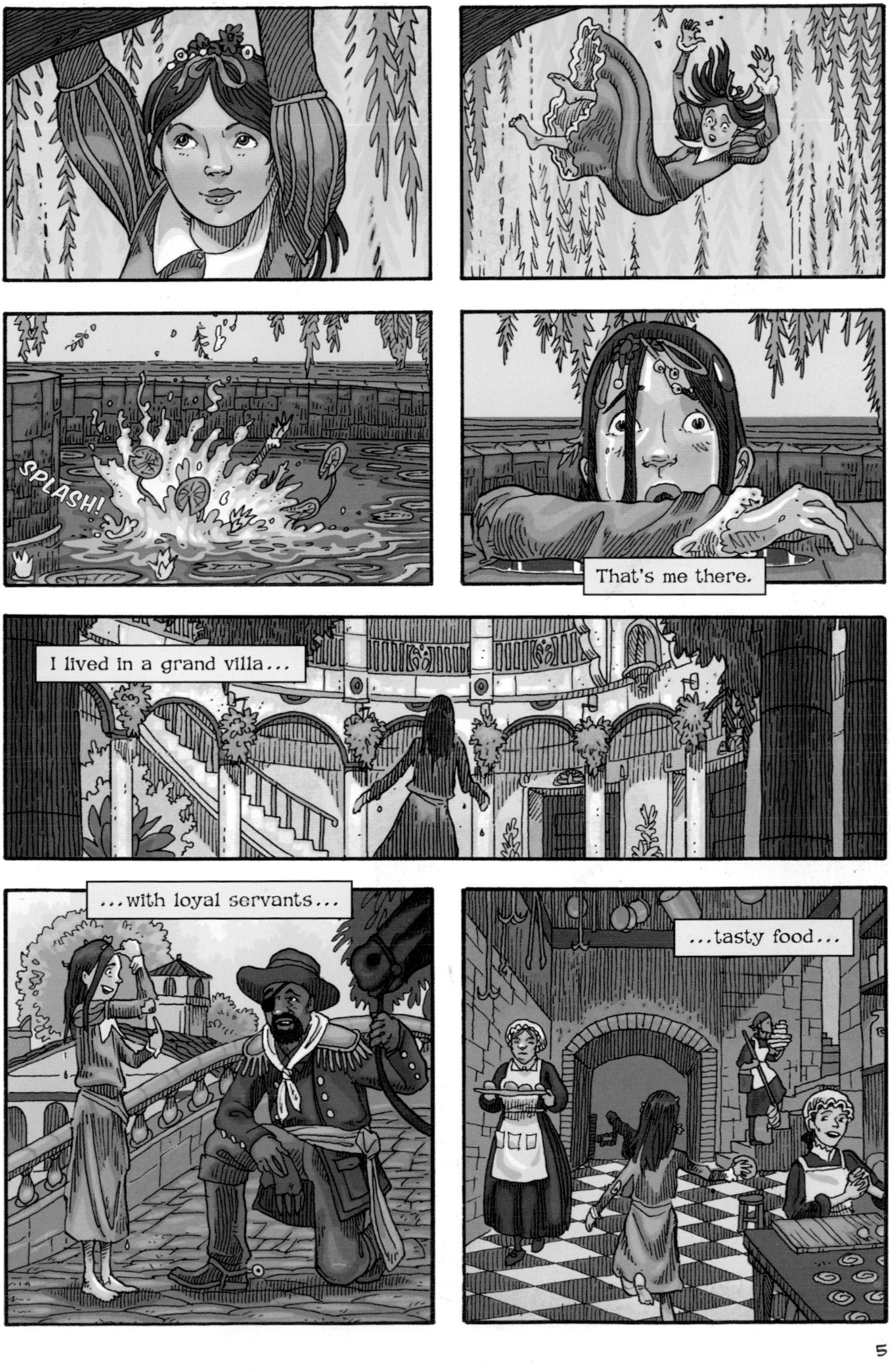
SPLASH!
That's me there.
I lived in a grand villa...
...with loyal servants...
...tasty food...

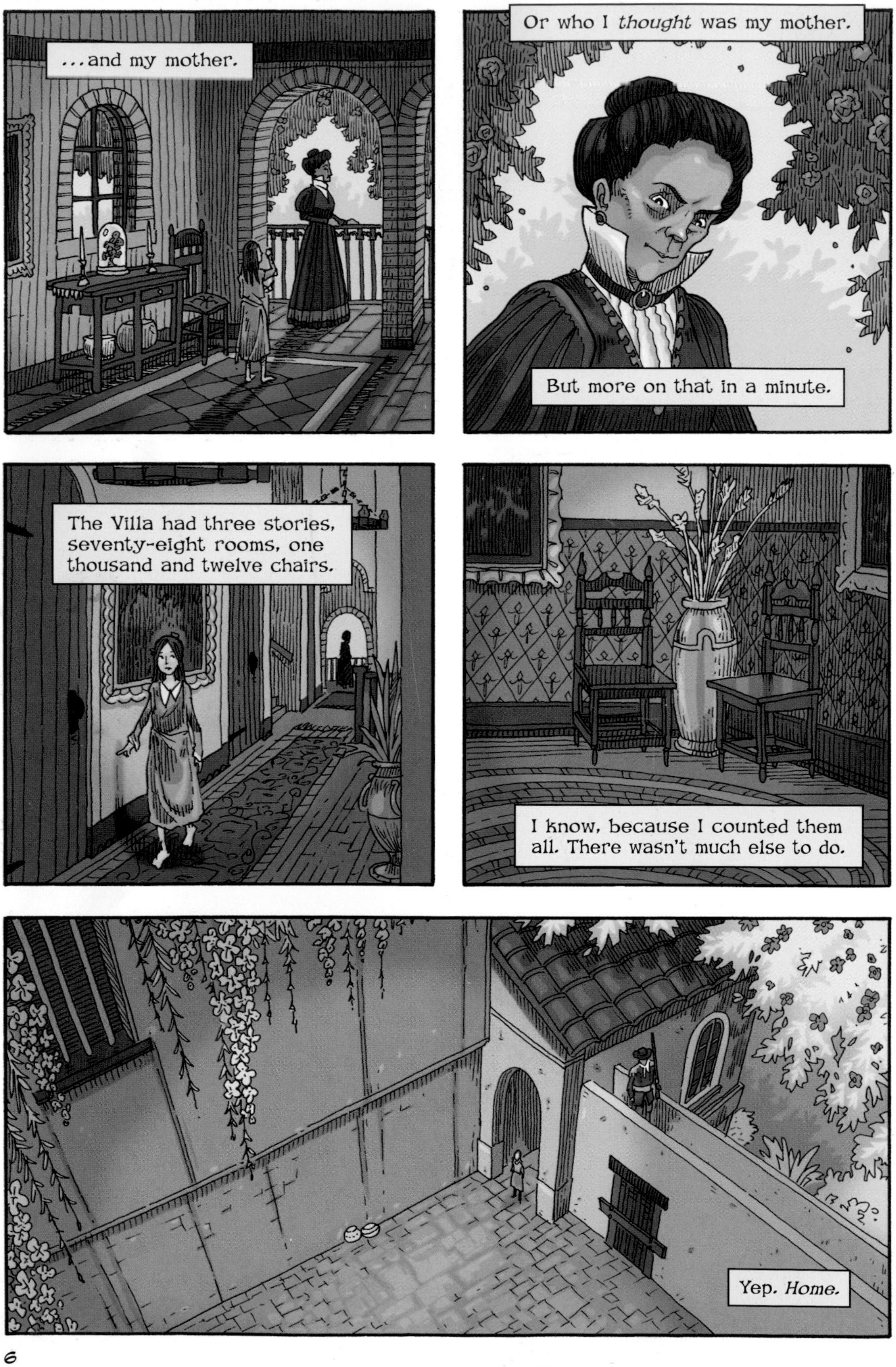
...and my mother.
Or who I *thought* was my mother.
But more on that in a minute.
The Villa had three stories, seventy-eight rooms, one thousand and twelve chairs.
I know, because I counted them all. There wasn't much else to do.
Yep. *Home.*

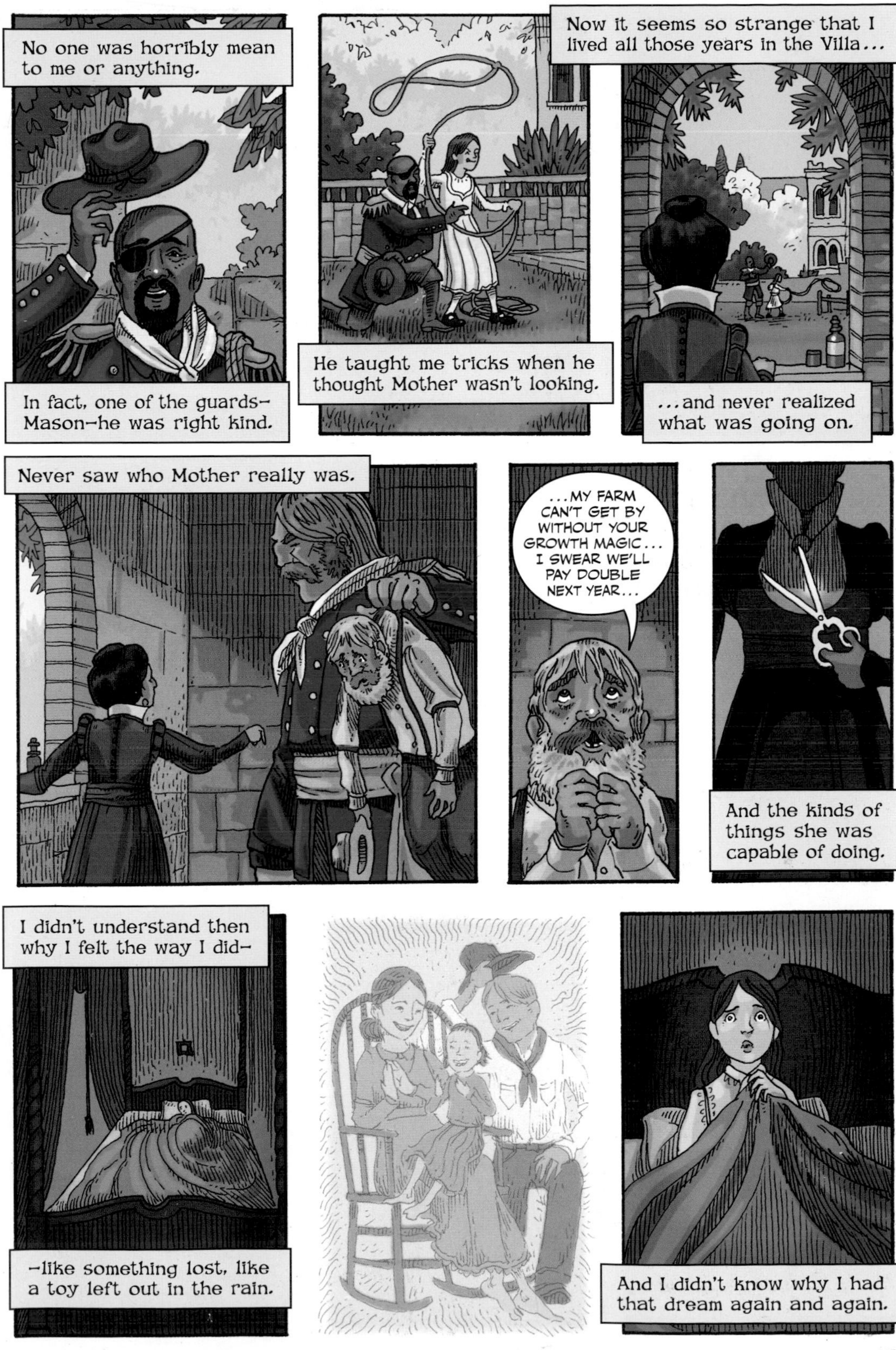
No one was horribly mean to me or anything.
In fact, one of the guards—Mason—he was right kind.
He taught me tricks when he thought Mother wasn't looking.
Now it seems so strange that I lived all those years in the Villa...
...and never realized what was going on.
Never saw who Mother really was.
...MY FARM CAN'T GET BY WITHOUT YOUR GROWTH MAGIC... I SWEAR WE'LL PAY DOUBLE NEXT YEAR...
And the kinds of things she was capable of doing.
I didn't understand then why I felt the way I did—
—like something lost, like a toy left out in the rain.
And I didn't know why I had that dream again and again.

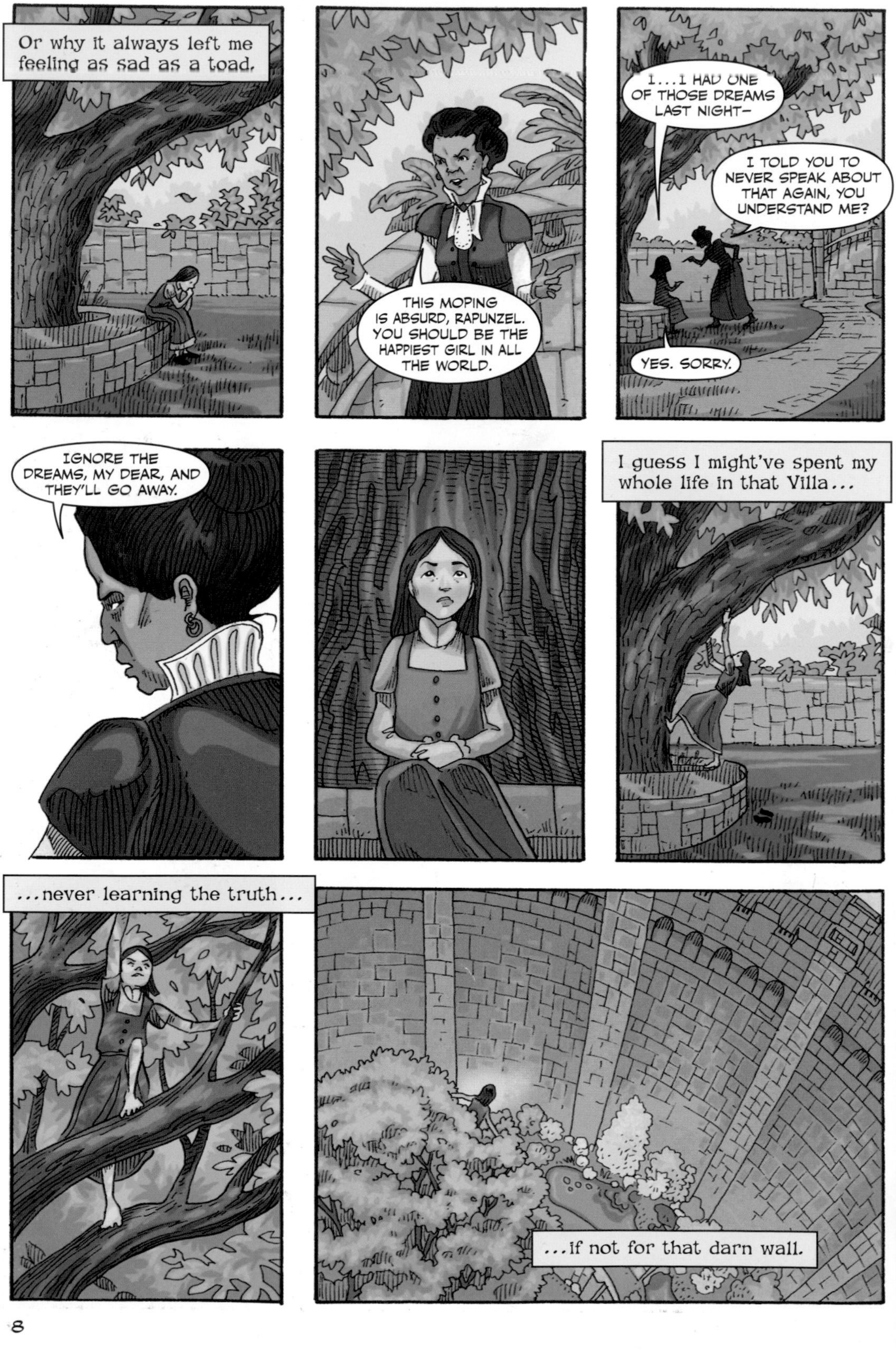
Or why it always left me feeling as sad as a toad.
THIS MOPING IS ABSURD, RAPUNZEL. YOU SHOULD BE THE HAPPIEST GIRL IN ALL THE WORLD.
I...I HAD ONE OF THOSE DREAMS LAST NIGHT–
I TOLD YOU TO NEVER SPEAK ABOUT THAT AGAIN, YOU UNDERSTAND ME?
YES. SORRY.
IGNORE THE DREAMS, MY DEAR, AND THEY'LL GO AWAY.
I guess I might've spent my whole life in that Villa...
...never learning the truth...
...if not for that darn wall.

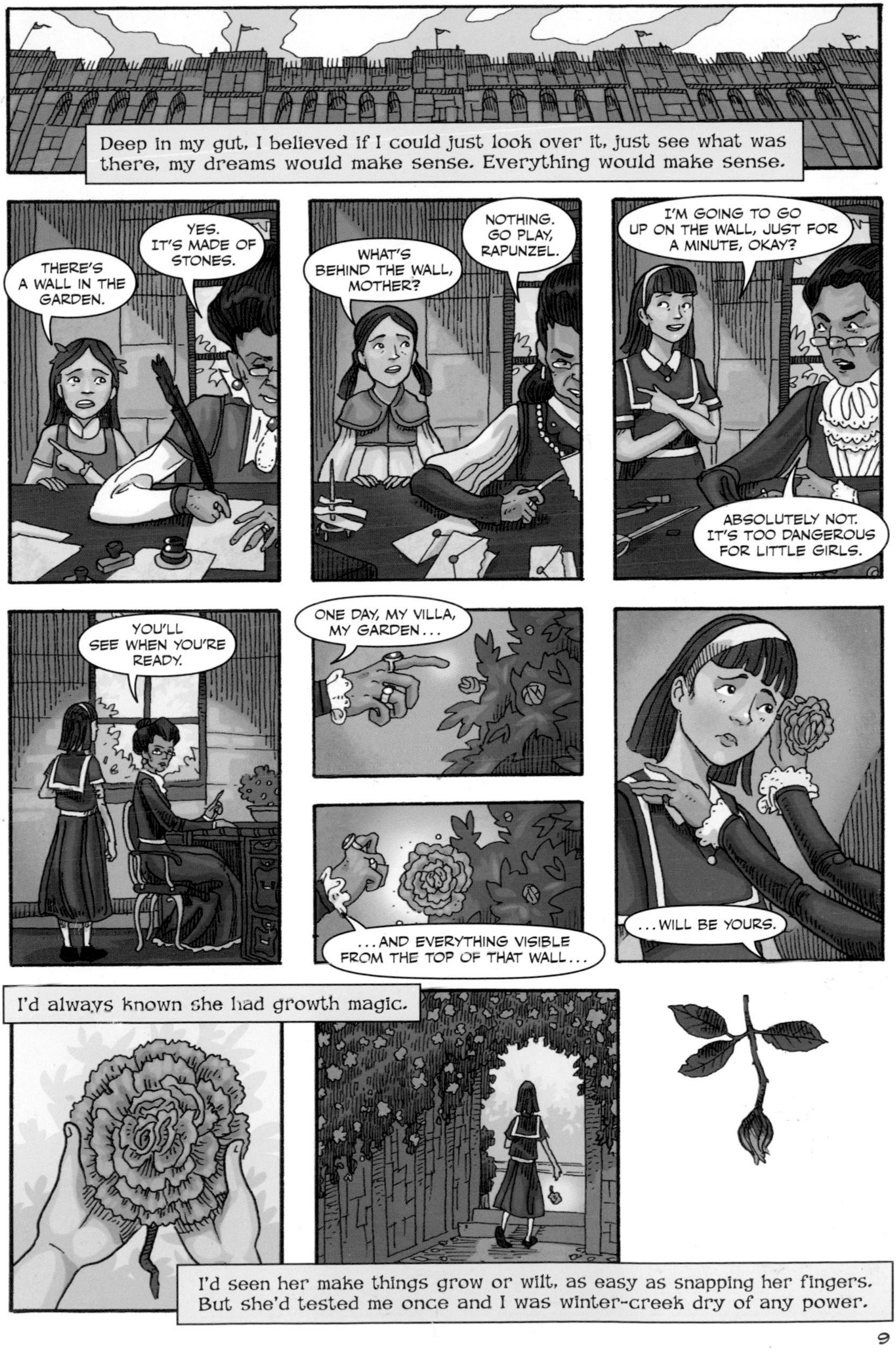

Deep in my gut, I believed if I could just look over it, just see what was there, my dreams would make sense. Everything would make sense.
THERE'S A WALL IN THE GARDEN.
YES. IT'S MADE OF STONES.
WHAT'S BEHIND THE WALL, MOTHER?
NOTHING. GO PLAY, RAPUNZEL.
I'M GOING TO GO UP ON THE WALL, JUST FOR A MINUTE, OKAY?
ABSOLUTELY NOT. IT'S TOO DANGEROUS FOR LITTLE GIRLS.
YOU'LL SEE WHEN YOU'RE READY.
ONE DAY, MY VILLA, MY GARDEN...
...AND EVERYTHING VISIBLE FROM THE TOP OF THAT WALL...
...WILL BE YOURS.
I'd always known she had growth magic.
I'd seen her make things grow or wilt, as easy as snapping her fingers. But she'd tested me once and I was winter-creek dry of any power.

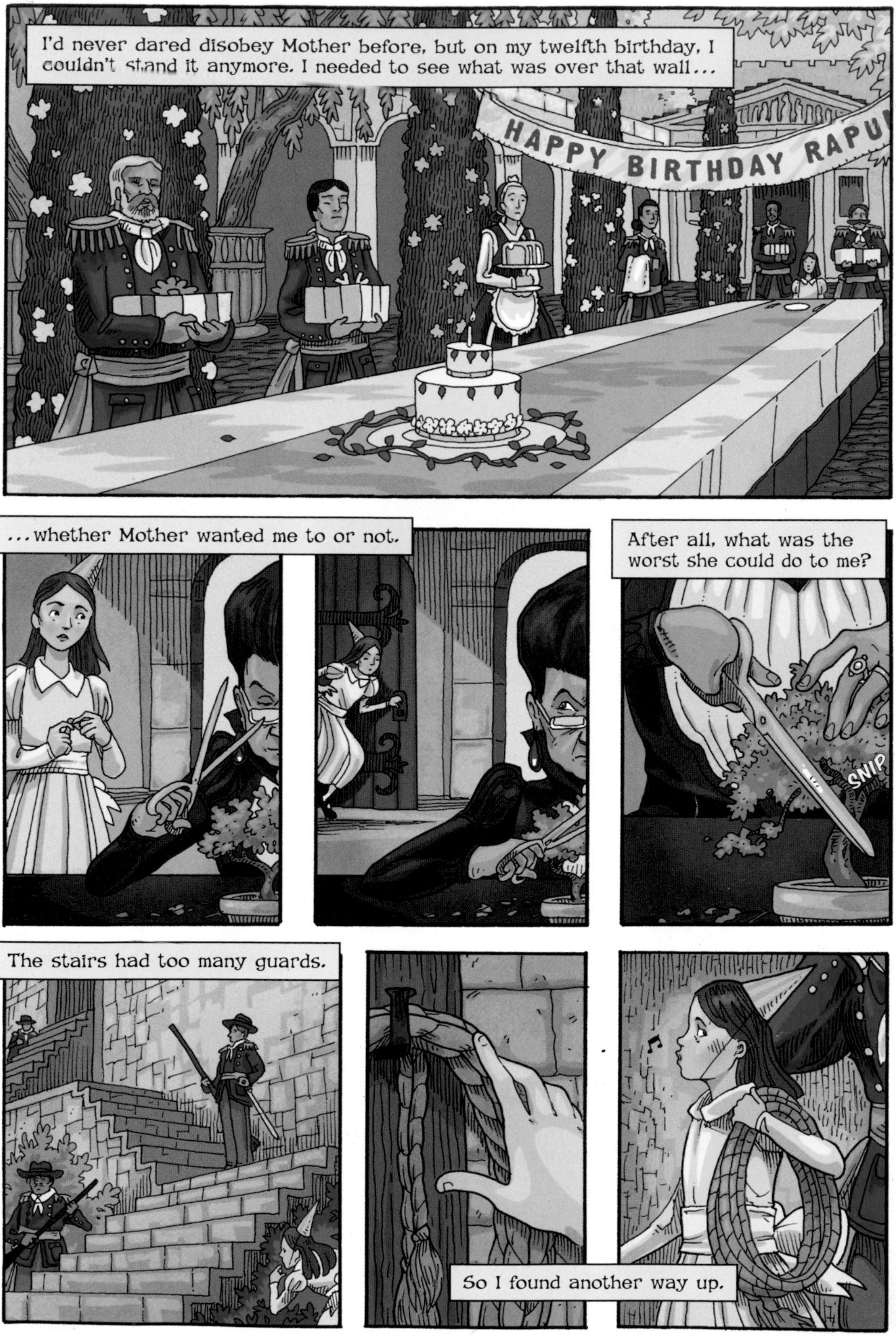
I'd never dared disobey Mother before, but on my twelfth birthday, I couldn't stand it anymore. I needed to see what was over that wall...
HAPPY BIRTHDAY RAPU
...whether Mother wanted me to or not.
After all, what was the worst she could do to me?
SNIP
The stairs had too many guards.
So I found another way up.

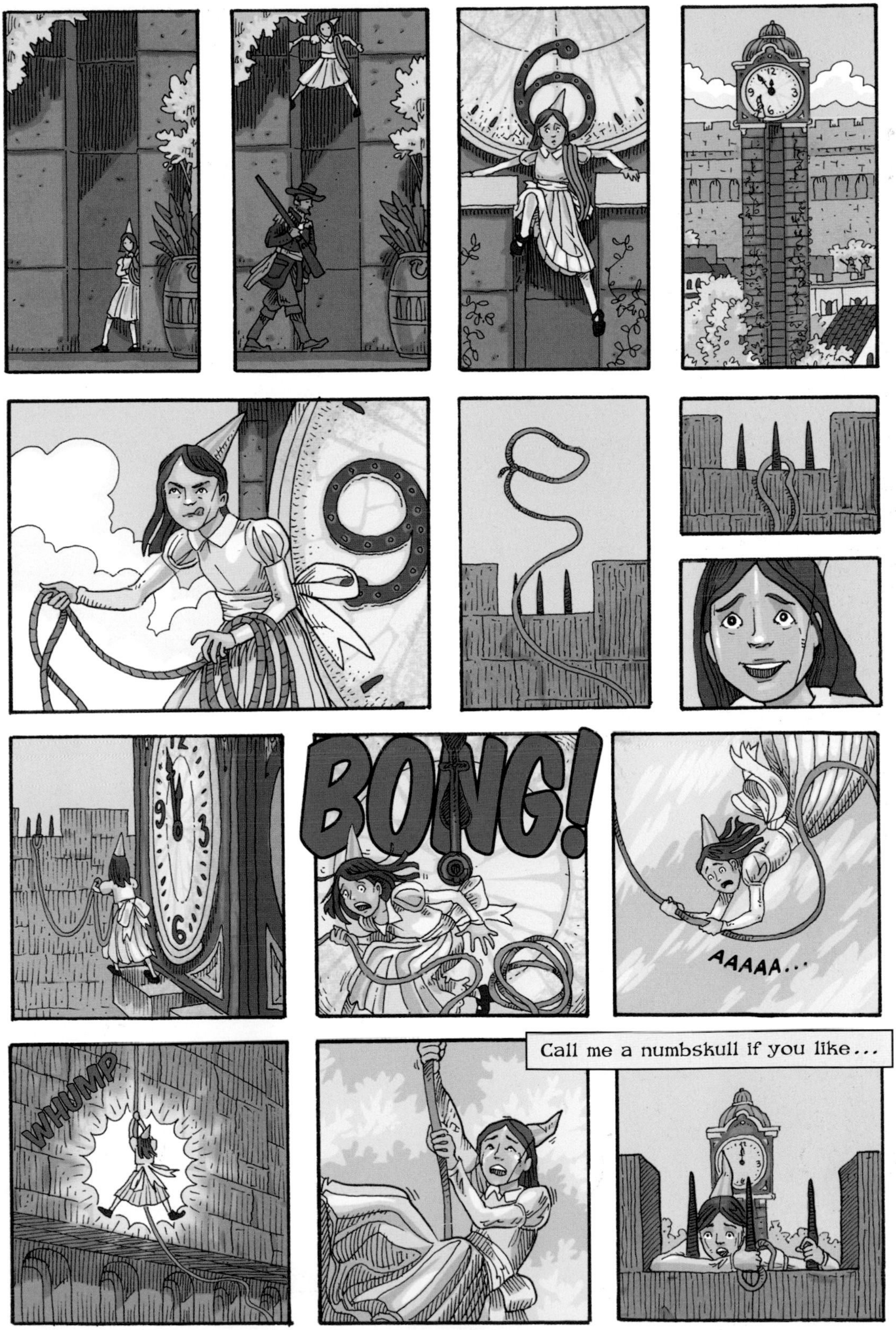
BONG!
AAAAA...
WHUMP
Call me a numbskull if you like...

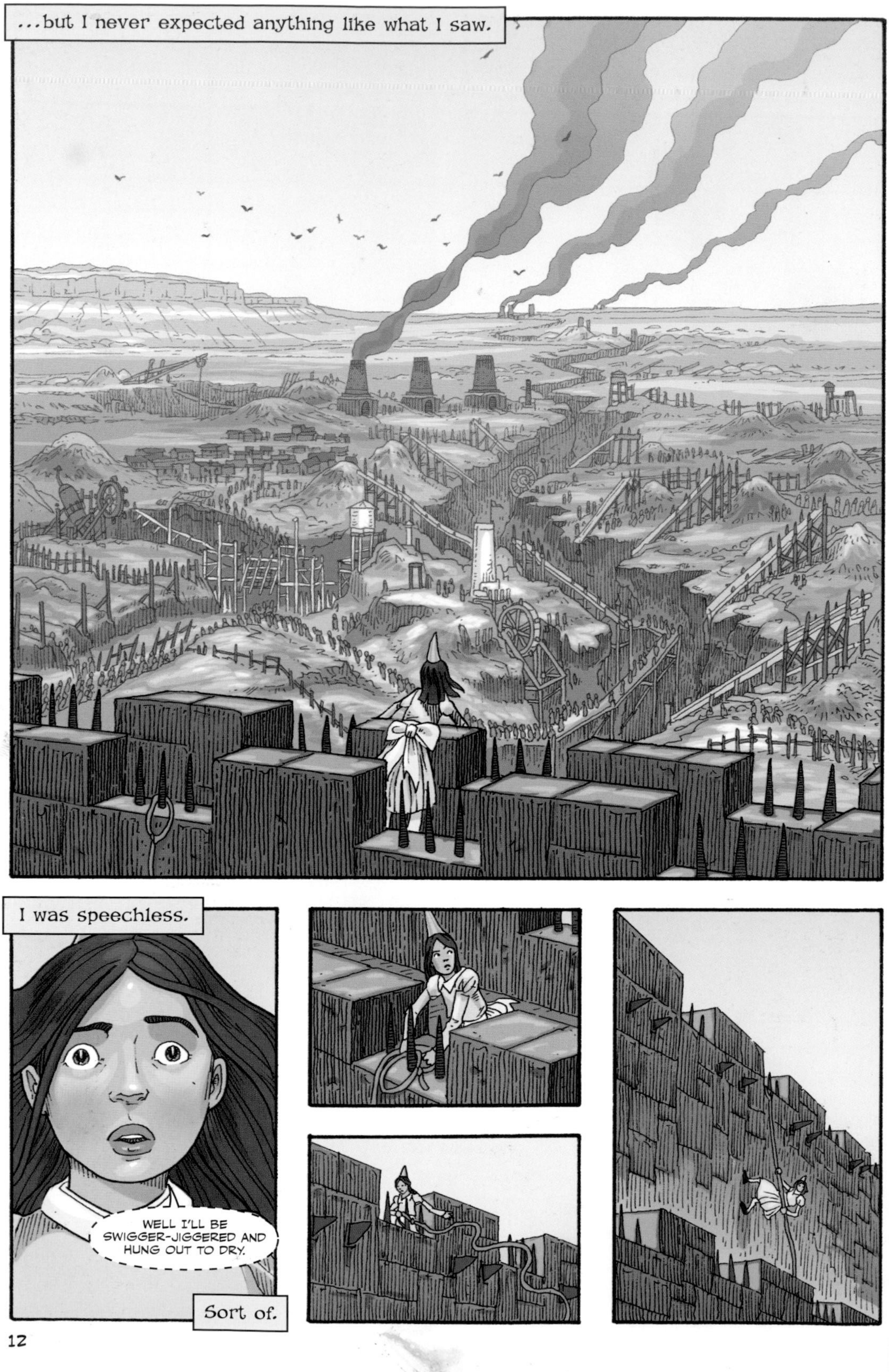
...but I never expected anything like what I saw.
I was speechless.
WELL I'LL BE SWIGGER-JIGGERED AND HUNG OUT TO DRY.
Sort of.

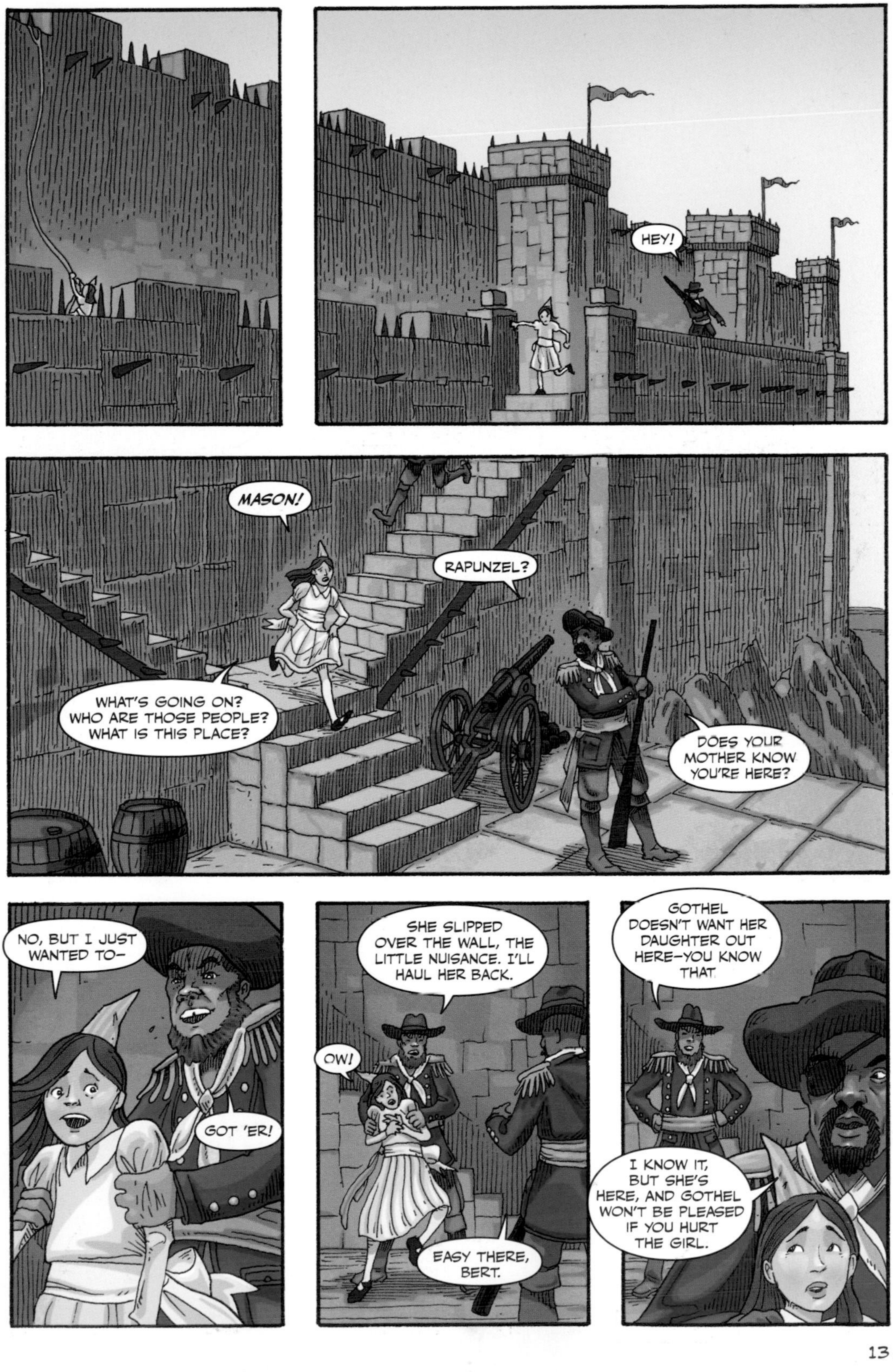
HEY!
MASON!
RAPUNZEL?
WHAT'S GOING ON? WHO ARE THOSE PEOPLE? WHAT IS THIS PLACE?
DOES YOUR MOTHER KNOW YOU'RE HERE?
NO, BUT I JUST WANTED TO–
GOT 'ER!
SHE SLIPPED OVER THE WALL, THE LITTLE NUISANCE. I'LL HAUL HER BACK.
OW!
EASY THERE, BERT.
GOTHEL DOESN'T WANT HER DAUGHTER OUT HERE–YOU KNOW THAT.
I KNOW IT, BUT SHE'S HERE, AND GOTHEL WON'T BE PLEASED IF YOU HURT THE GIRL.

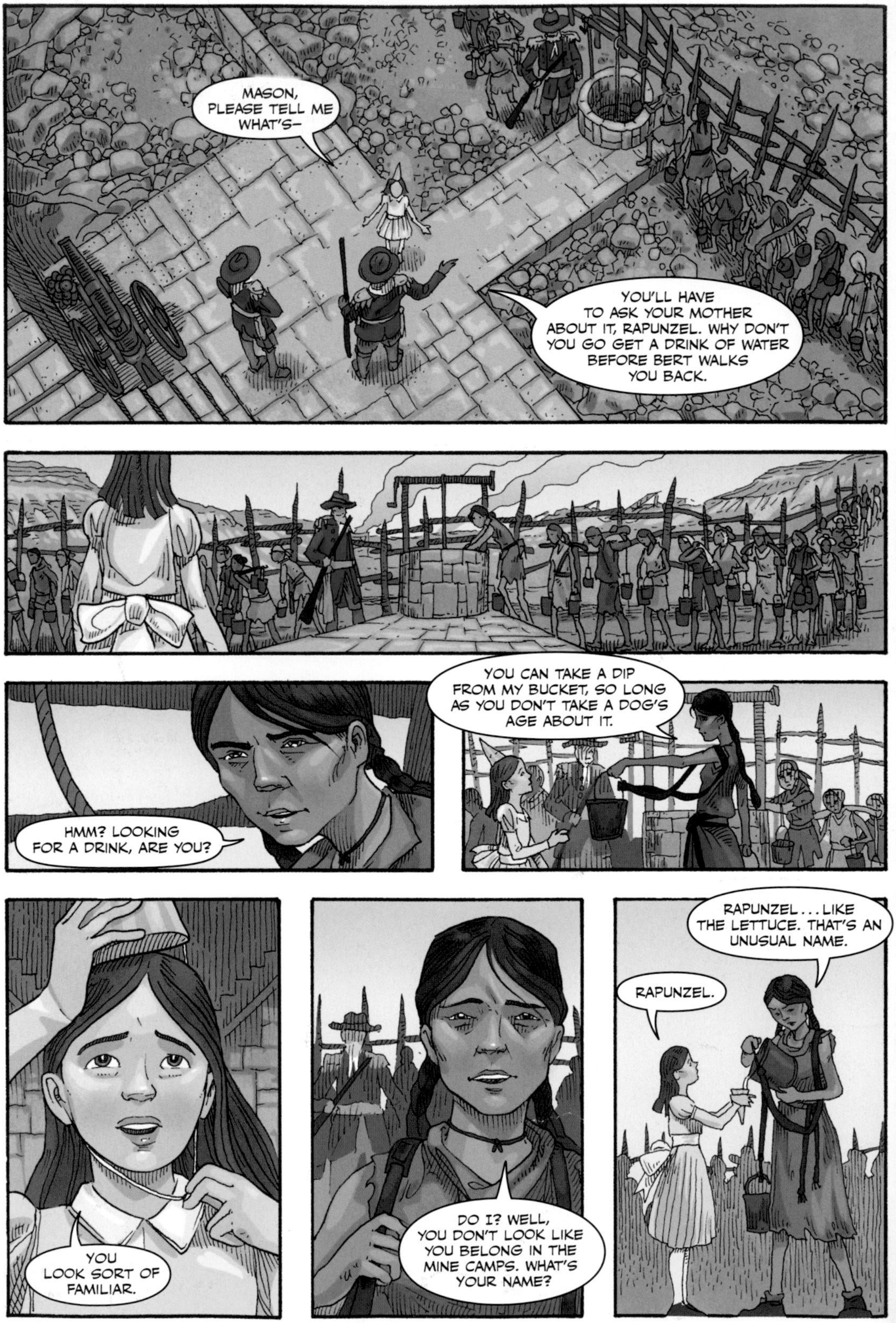
MASON, PLEASE TELL ME WHAT'S—
YOU'LL HAVE TO ASK YOUR MOTHER ABOUT IT, RAPUNZEL. WHY DON'T YOU GO GET A DRINK OF WATER BEFORE BERT WALKS YOU BACK.
HMM? LOOKING FOR A DRINK, ARE YOU?
YOU CAN TAKE A DIP FROM MY BUCKET, SO LONG AS YOU DON'T TAKE A DOG'S AGE ABOUT IT.
YOU LOOK SORT OF FAMILIAR.
DO I? WELL, YOU DON'T LOOK LIKE YOU BELONG IN THE MINE CAMPS. WHAT'S YOUR NAME?
RAPUNZEL.
RAPUNZEL... LIKE THE LETTUCE. THAT'S AN UNUSUAL NAME.

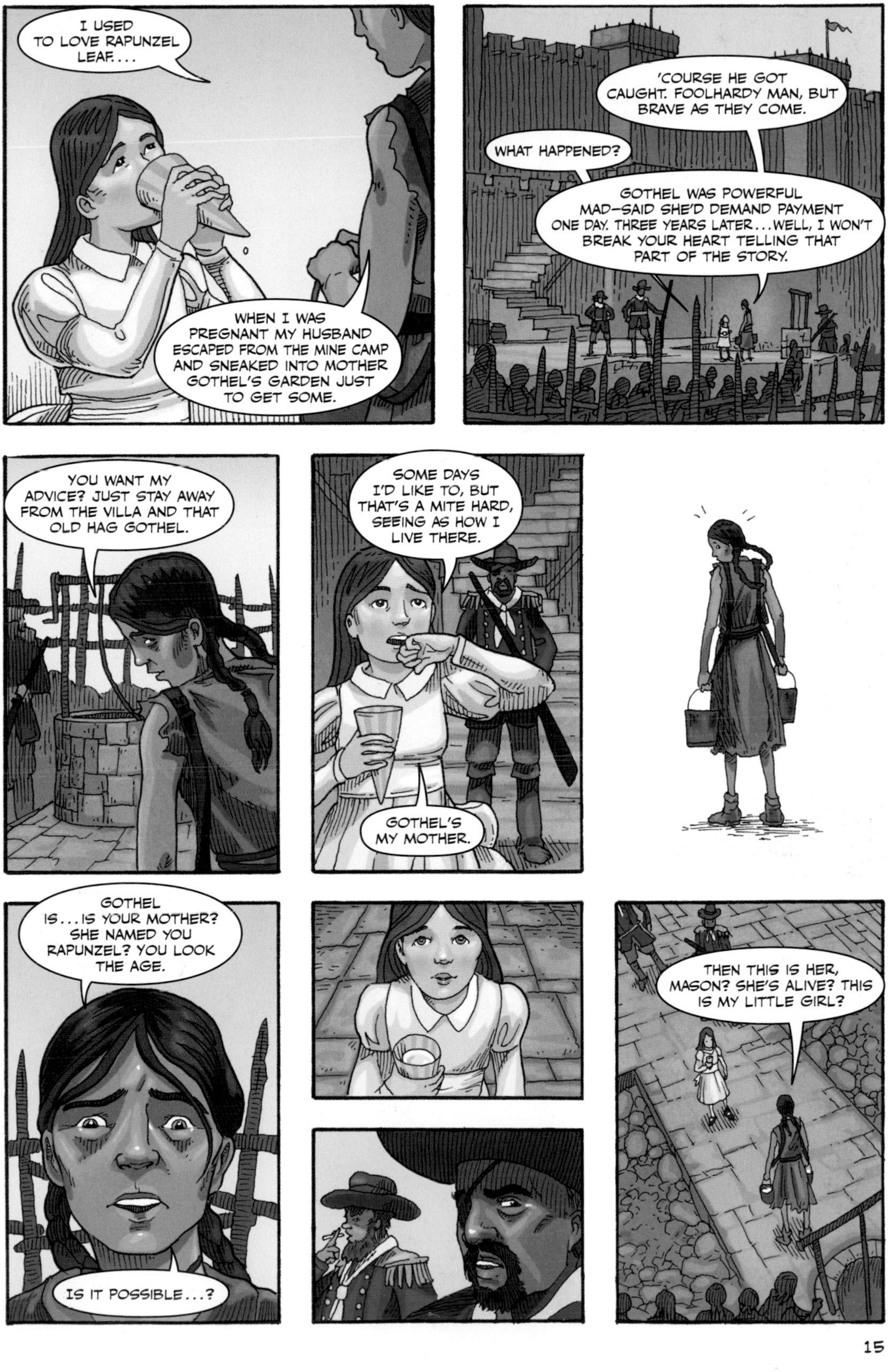
I USED TO LOVE RAPUNZEL LEAF....
WHEN I WAS PREGNANT MY HUSBAND ESCAPED FROM THE MINE CAMP AND SNEAKED INTO MOTHER GOTHEL'S GARDEN JUST TO GET SOME.
'COURSE HE GOT CAUGHT. FOOLHARDY MAN, BUT BRAVE AS THEY COME.
WHAT HAPPENED?
GOTHEL WAS POWERFUL MAD—SAID SHE'D DEMAND PAYMENT ONE DAY. THREE YEARS LATER...WELL, I WON'T BREAK YOUR HEART TELLING THAT PART OF THE STORY.
YOU WANT MY ADVICE? JUST STAY AWAY FROM THE VILLA AND THAT OLD HAG GOTHEL.
SOME DAYS I'D LIKE TO, BUT THAT'S A MITE HARD, SEEING AS HOW I LIVE THERE.
GOTHEL'S MY MOTHER.
GOTHEL IS...IS YOUR MOTHER? SHE NAMED YOU RAPUNZEL? YOU LOOK THE AGE.
IS IT POSSIBLE...?
THEN THIS IS HER, MASON? SHE'S ALIVE? THIS IS MY LITTLE GIRL?

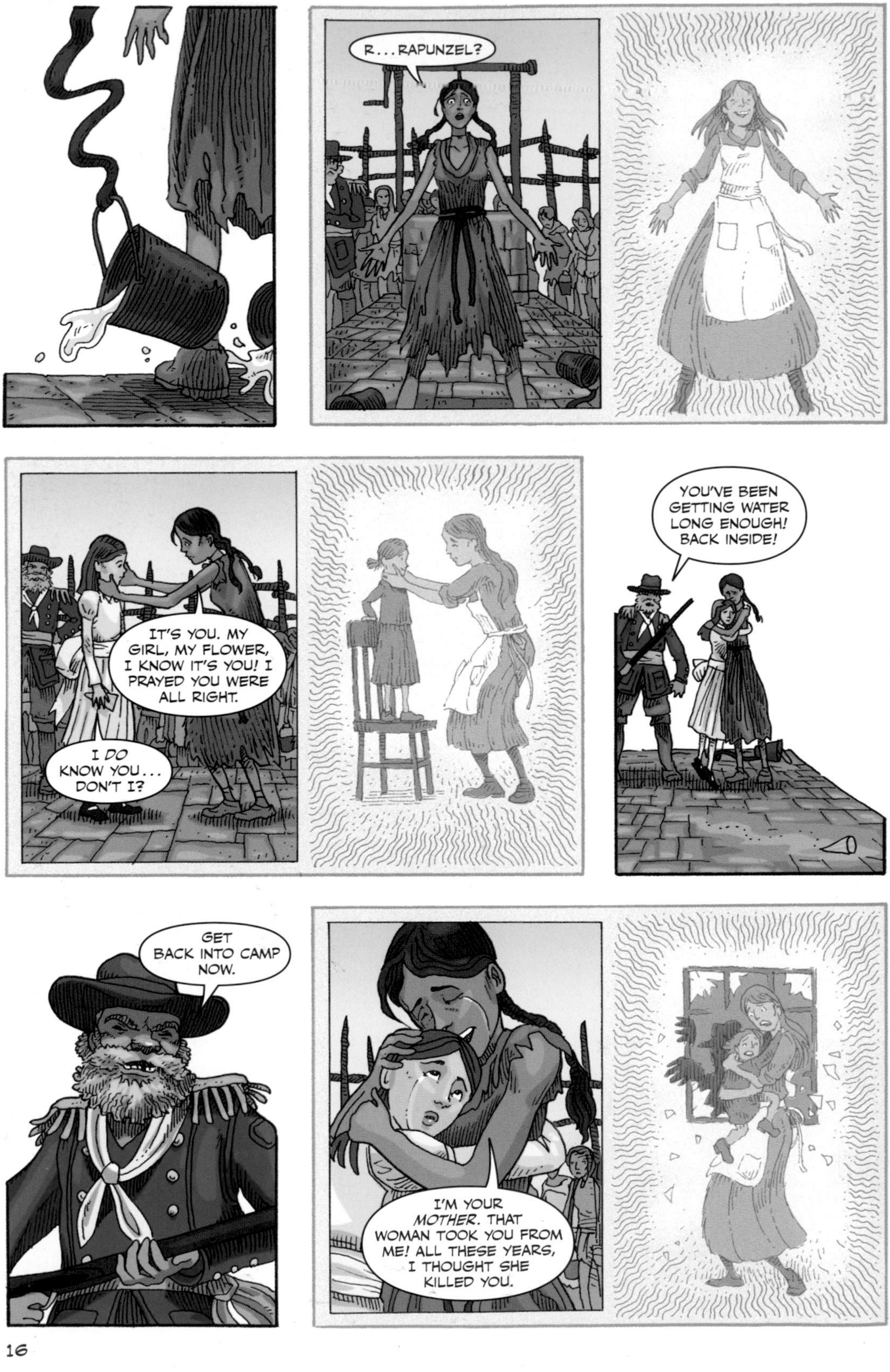
R...RAPUNZEL?
IT'S YOU. MY GIRL, MY FLOWER, I KNOW IT'S YOU! I PRAYED YOU WERE ALL RIGHT.
I *DO* KNOW YOU... DON'T I?
YOU'VE BEEN GETTING WATER LONG ENOUGH! BACK INSIDE!
GET BACK INTO CAMP NOW.
I'M YOUR *MOTHER*. THAT WOMAN TOOK YOU FROM ME! ALL THESE YEARS, I THOUGHT SHE KILLED YOU.

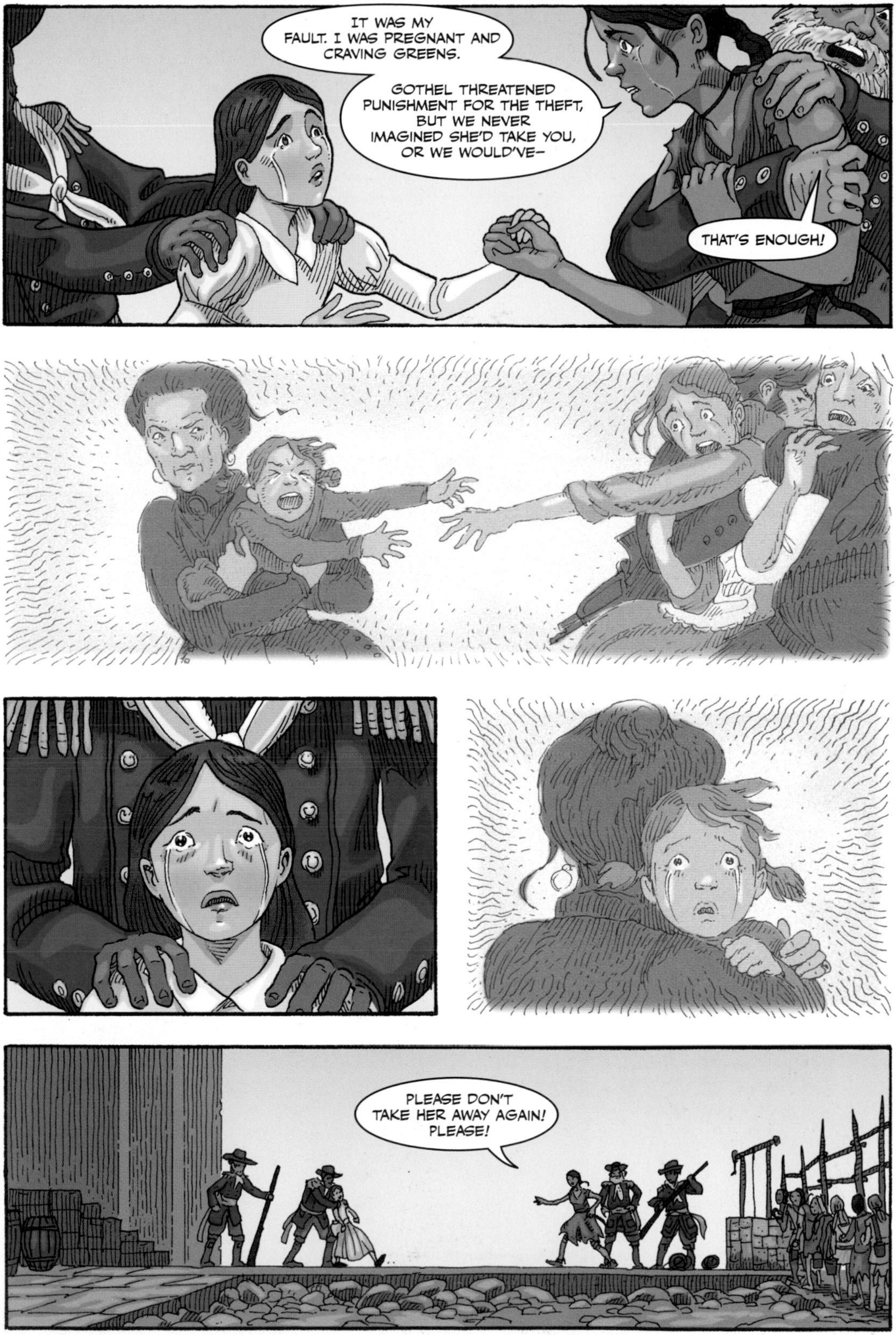
IT WAS MY FAULT. I WAS PREGNANT AND CRAVING GREENS.
GOTHEL THREATENED PUNISHMENT FOR THE THEFT, BUT WE NEVER IMAGINED SHE'D TAKE YOU, OR WE WOULD'VE–
THAT'S ENOUGH!
PLEASE DON'T TAKE HER AWAY AGAIN! PLEASE!

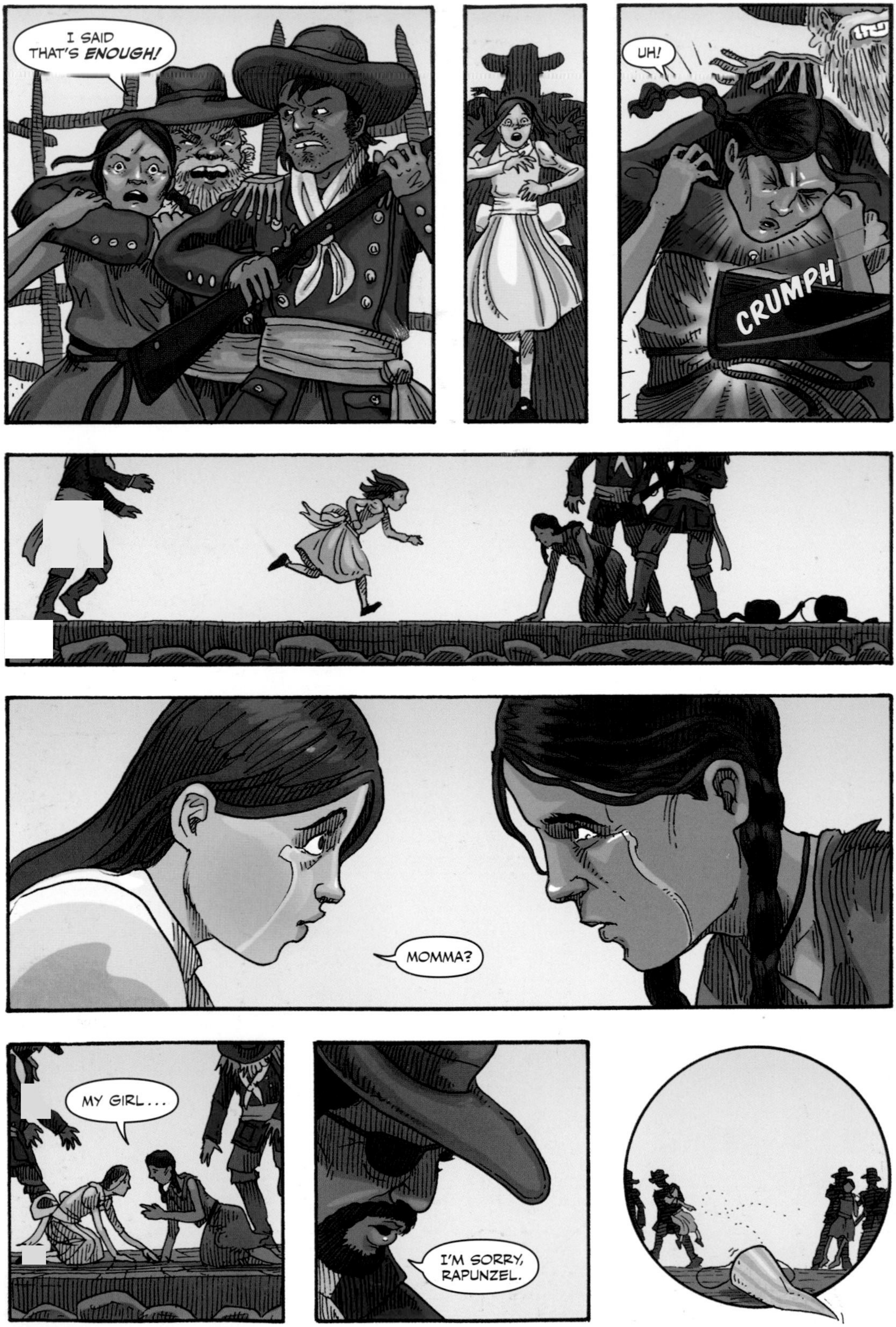
I SAID THAT'S ENOUGH!
UH!
CRUMPH
MOMMA?
MY GIRL...
I'M SORRY, RAPUNZEL.

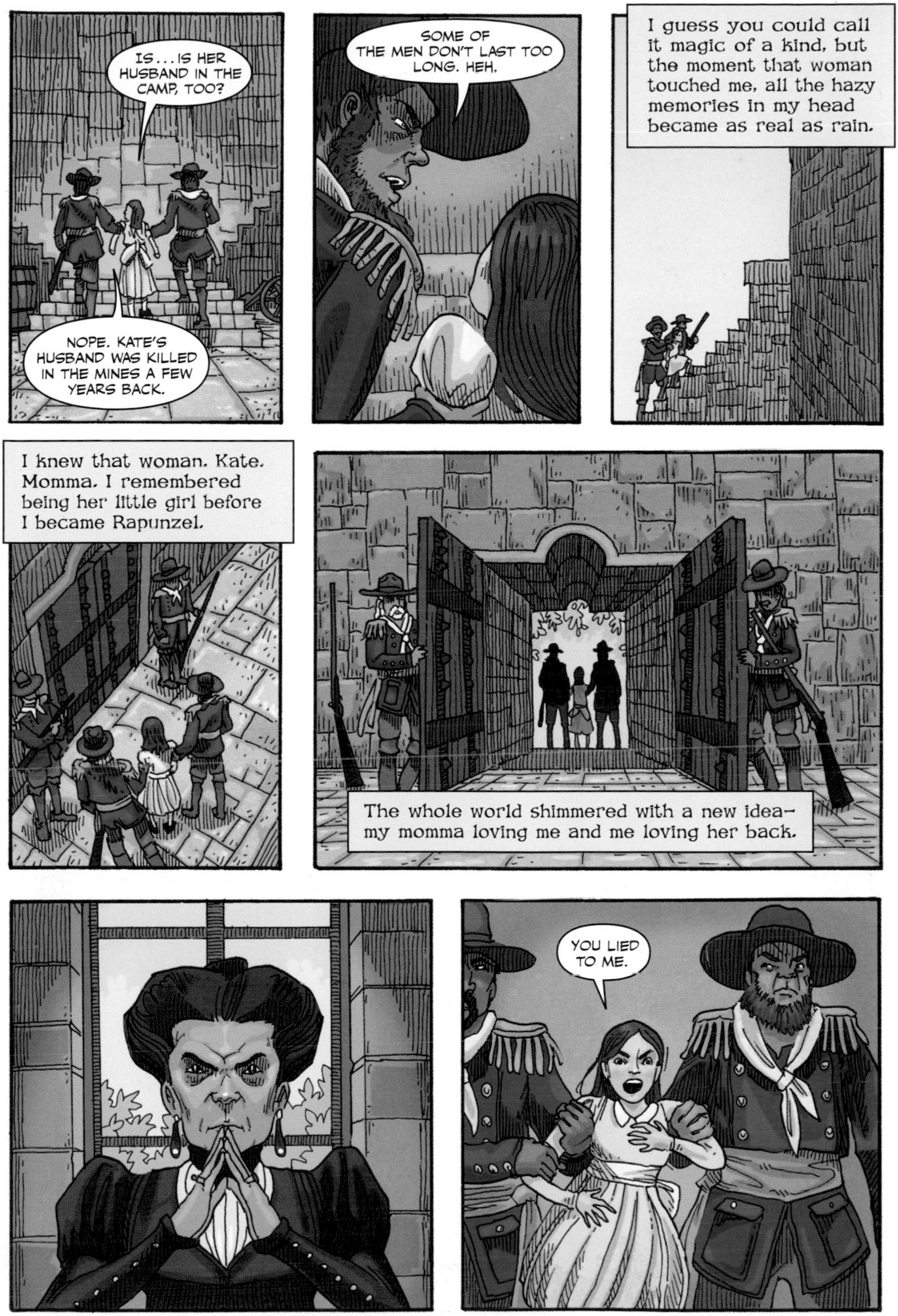

IS...IS HER HUSBAND IN THE CAMP, TOO?
NOPE. KATE'S HUSBAND WAS KILLED IN THE MINES A FEW YEARS BACK.
SOME OF THE MEN DON'T LAST TOO LONG. HEH.
I guess you could call it magic of a kind, but the moment that woman touched me, all the hazy memories in my head became as real as rain.
I knew that woman. Kate. Momma. I remembered being her little girl before I became Rapunzel.
The whole world shimmered with a new idea– my momma loving me and me loving her back.
YOU LIED TO ME.

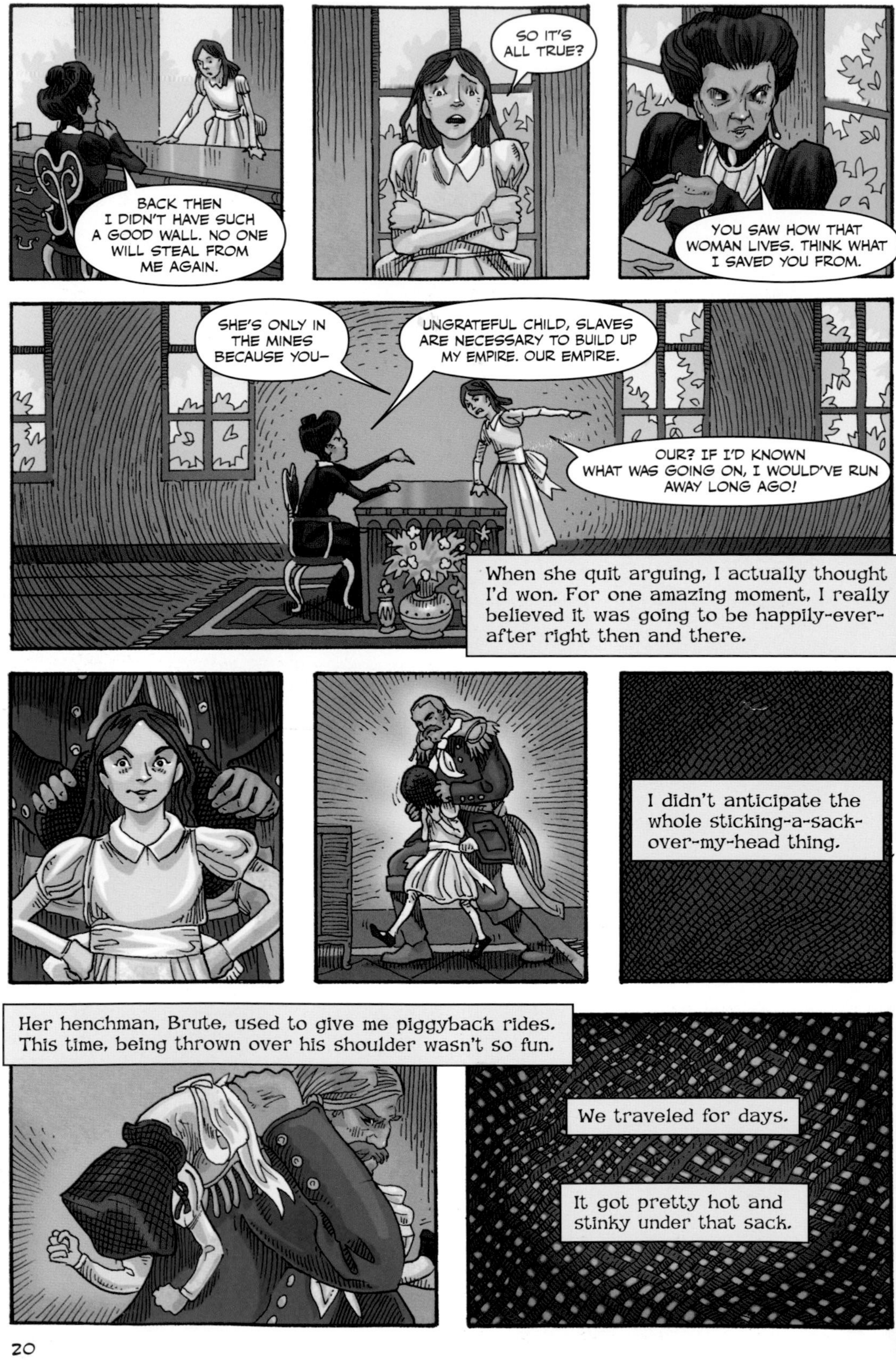
BACK THEN I DIDN'T HAVE SUCH A GOOD WALL. NO ONE WILL STEAL FROM ME AGAIN.
SO IT'S ALL TRUE?
YOU SAW HOW THAT WOMAN LIVES. THINK WHAT I SAVED YOU FROM.
SHE'S ONLY IN THE MINES BECAUSE YOU–
UNGRATEFUL CHILD, SLAVES ARE NECESSARY TO BUILD UP MY EMPIRE. OUR EMPIRE.
OUR? IF I'D KNOWN WHAT WAS GOING ON, I WOULD'VE RUN AWAY LONG AGO!
When she quit arguing, I actually thought I'd won. For one amazing moment, I really believed it was going to be happily-ever-after right then and there.
I didn't anticipate the whole sticking-a-sack-over-my-head thing.
Her henchman, Brute, used to give me piggyback rides. This time, being thrown over his shoulder wasn't so fun.
We traveled for days.
It got pretty hot and stinky under that sack.

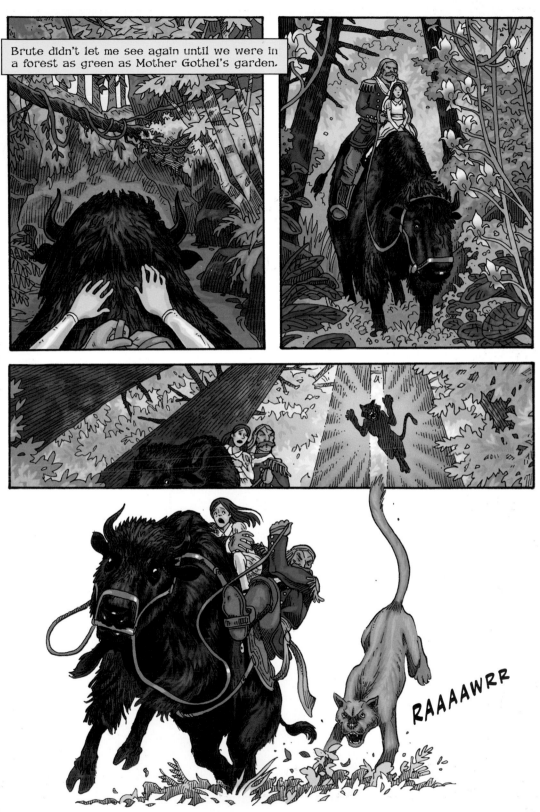

Brute didn't let me see again until we were in a forest as green as Mother Gothel's garden.

RAAAAWRR

21

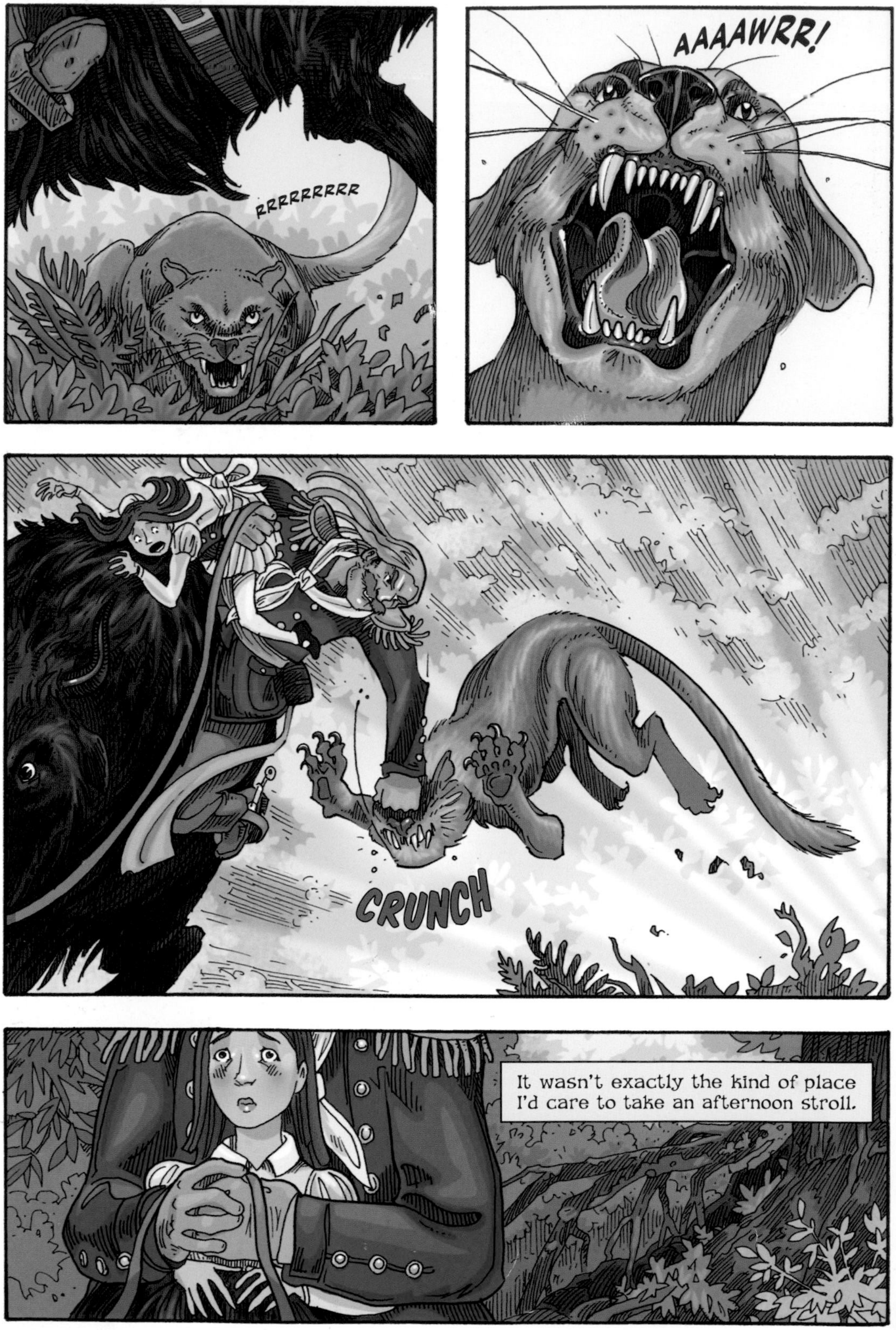
RRRRRRRRR
AAAAWRR!
CRUNCH
It wasn't exactly the kind of place I'd care to take an afternoon stroll.

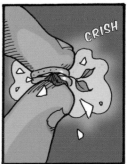

CRISH

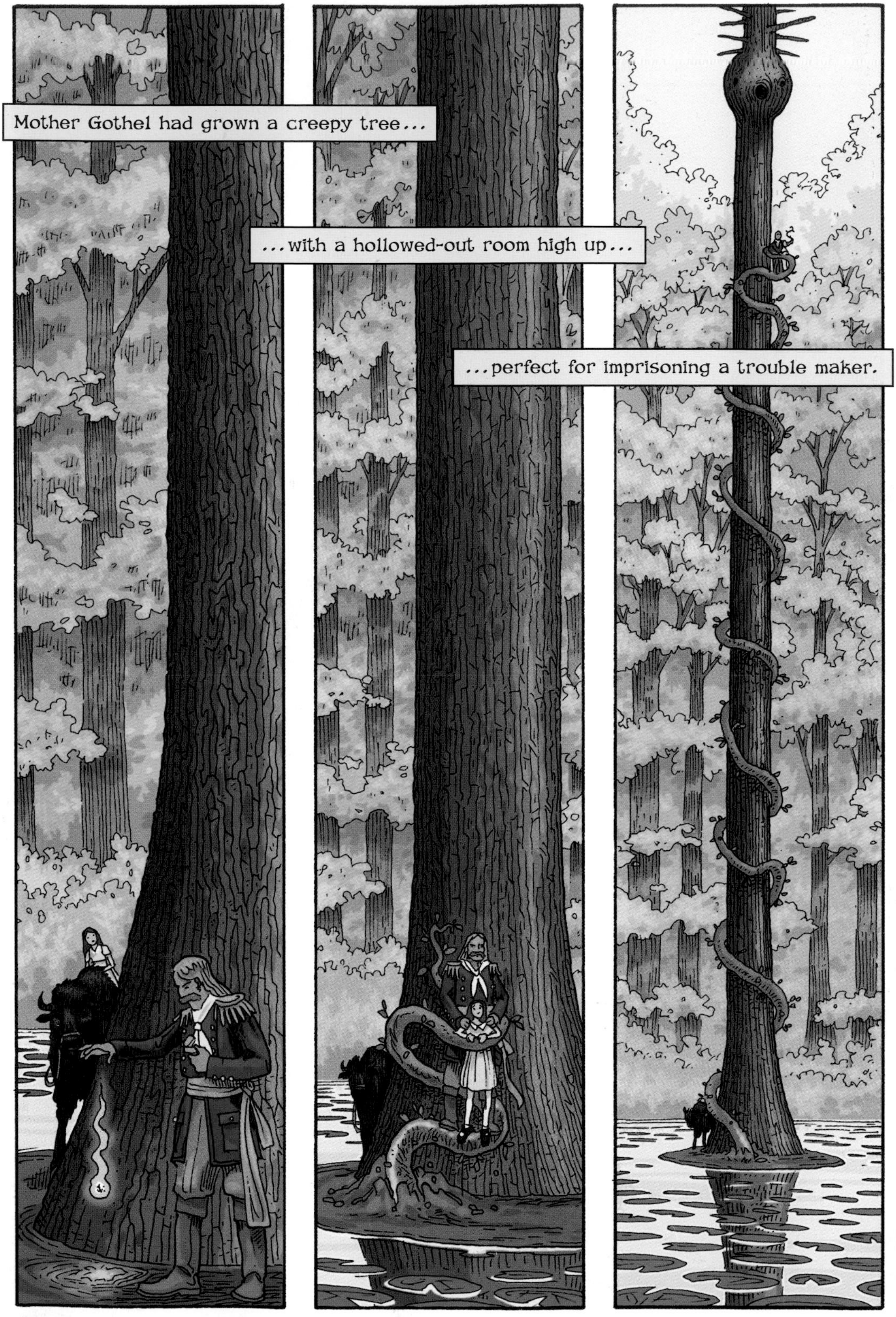
Mother Gothel had grown a creepy tree...
...with a hollowed-out room high up...
...perfect for imprisoning a trouble maker.

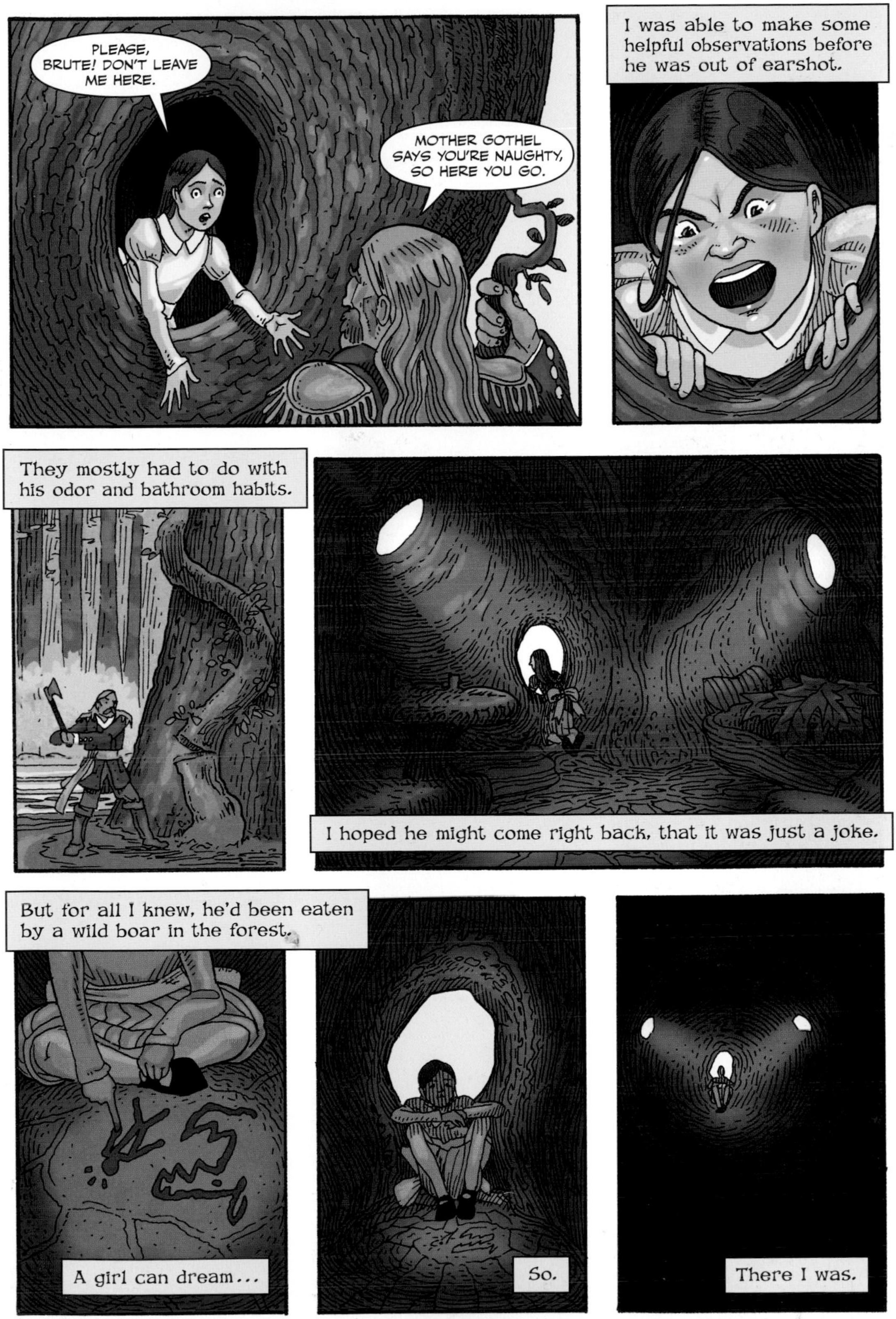
PLEASE, BRUTE! DON'T LEAVE ME HERE.
MOTHER GOTHEL SAYS YOU'RE NAUGHTY, SO HERE YOU GO.
I was able to make some helpful observations before he was out of earshot.
They mostly had to do with his odor and bathroom habits.
I hoped he might come right back, that it was just a joke.
But for all I knew, he'd been eaten by a wild boar in the forest.
A girl can dream...
So.
There I was.

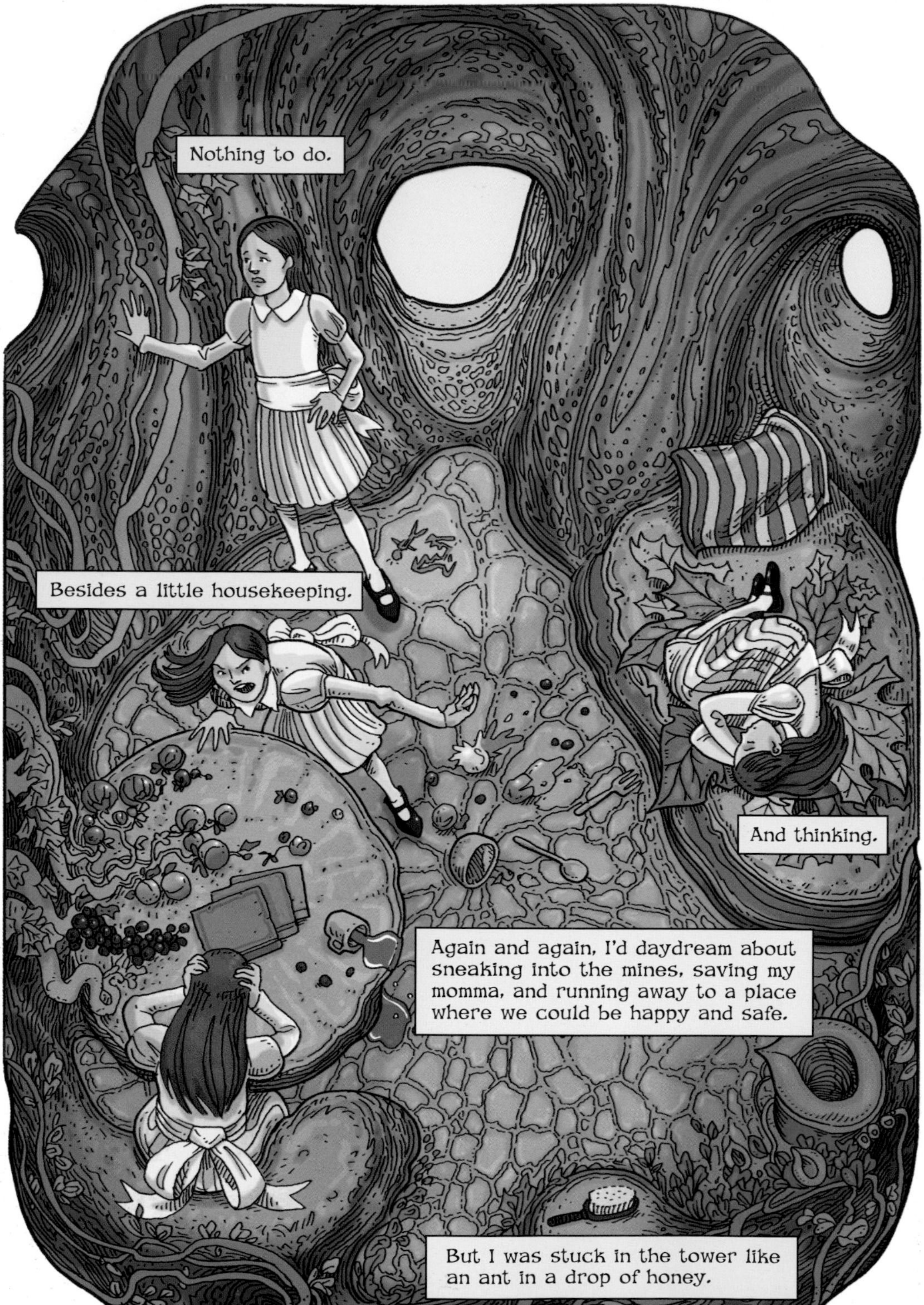
Nothing to do.
Besides a little housekeeping.
And thinking.
Again and again, I'd daydream about sneaking into the mines, saving my momma, and running away to a place where we could be happy and safe.
But I was stuck in the tower like an ant in a drop of honey.

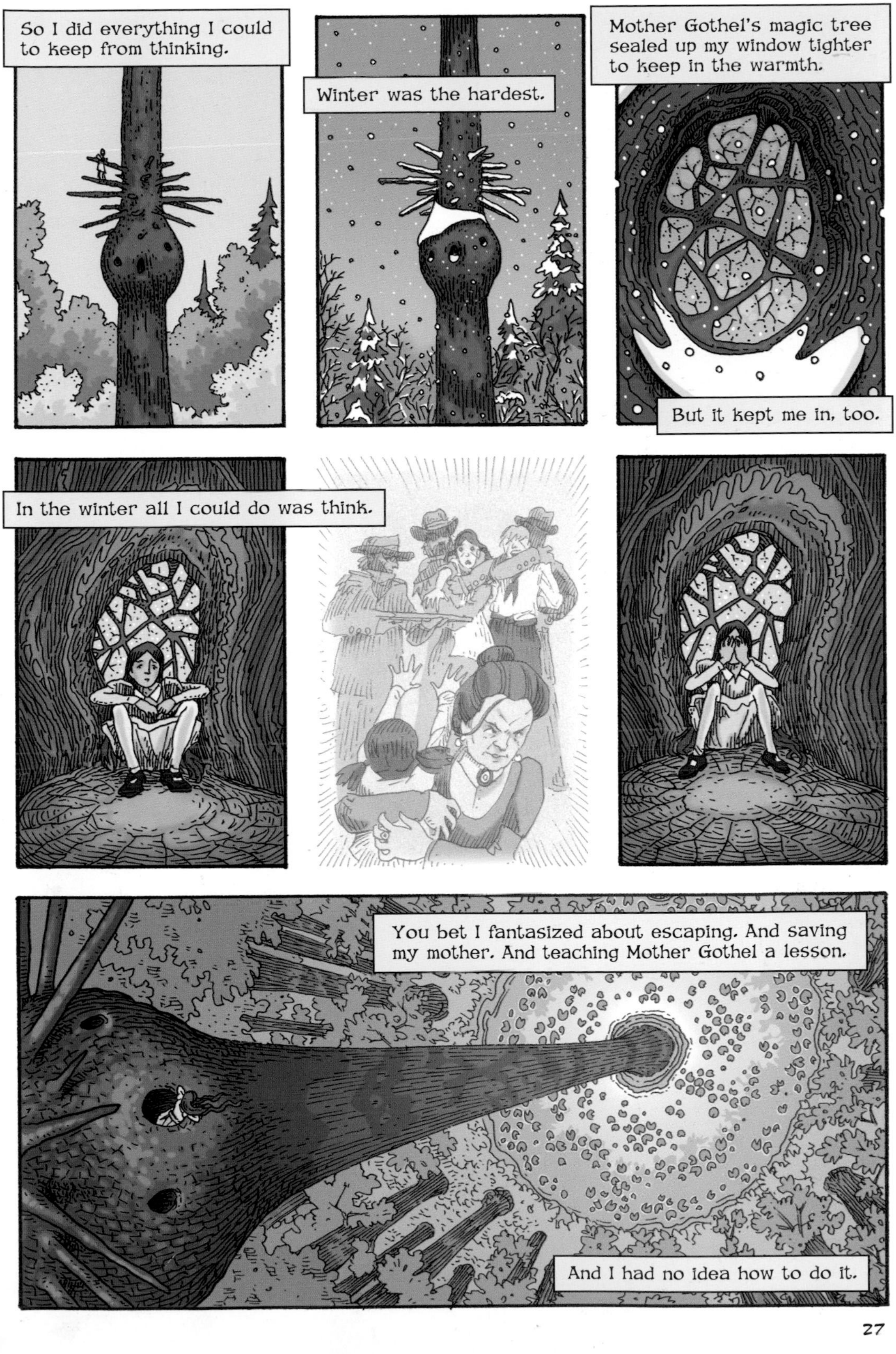
So I did everything I could to keep from thinking.
Winter was the hardest.
Mother Gothel's magic tree sealed up my window tighter to keep in the warmth.
But it kept me in, too.
In the winter all I could do was think.
You bet I fantasized about escaping. And saving my mother. And teaching Mother Gothel a lesson.
And I had no idea how to do it.

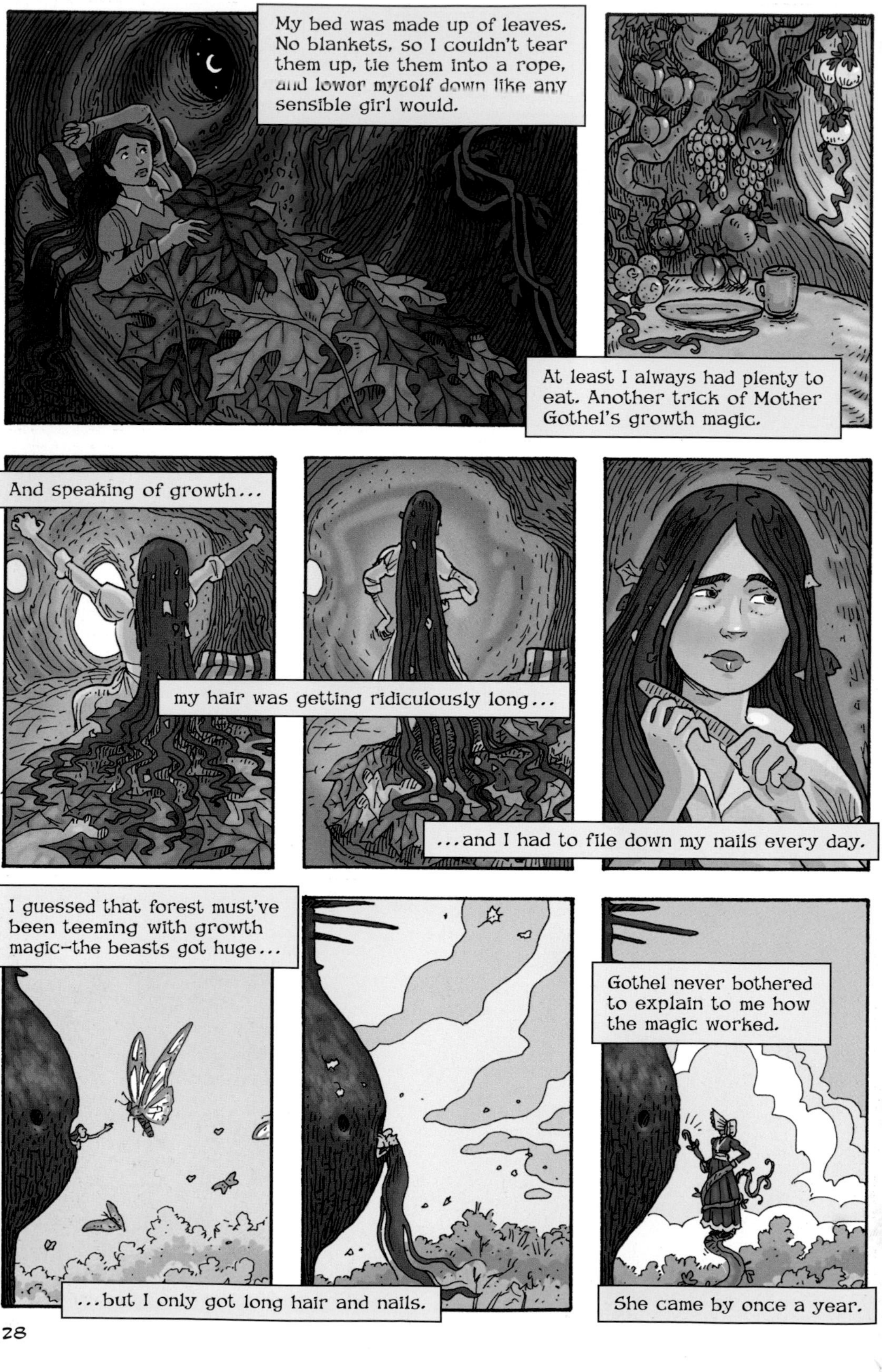
My bed was made up of leaves. No blankets, so I couldn't tear them up, tie them into a rope, and lower myself down like any sensible girl would.
At least I always had plenty to eat. Another trick of Mother Gothel's growth magic.
And speaking of growth...
my hair was getting ridiculously long...
...and I had to file down my nails every day.
I guessed that forest must've been teeming with growth magic—the beasts got huge...
...but I only got long hair and nails.
Gothel never bothered to explain to me how the magic worked.
She came by once a year.

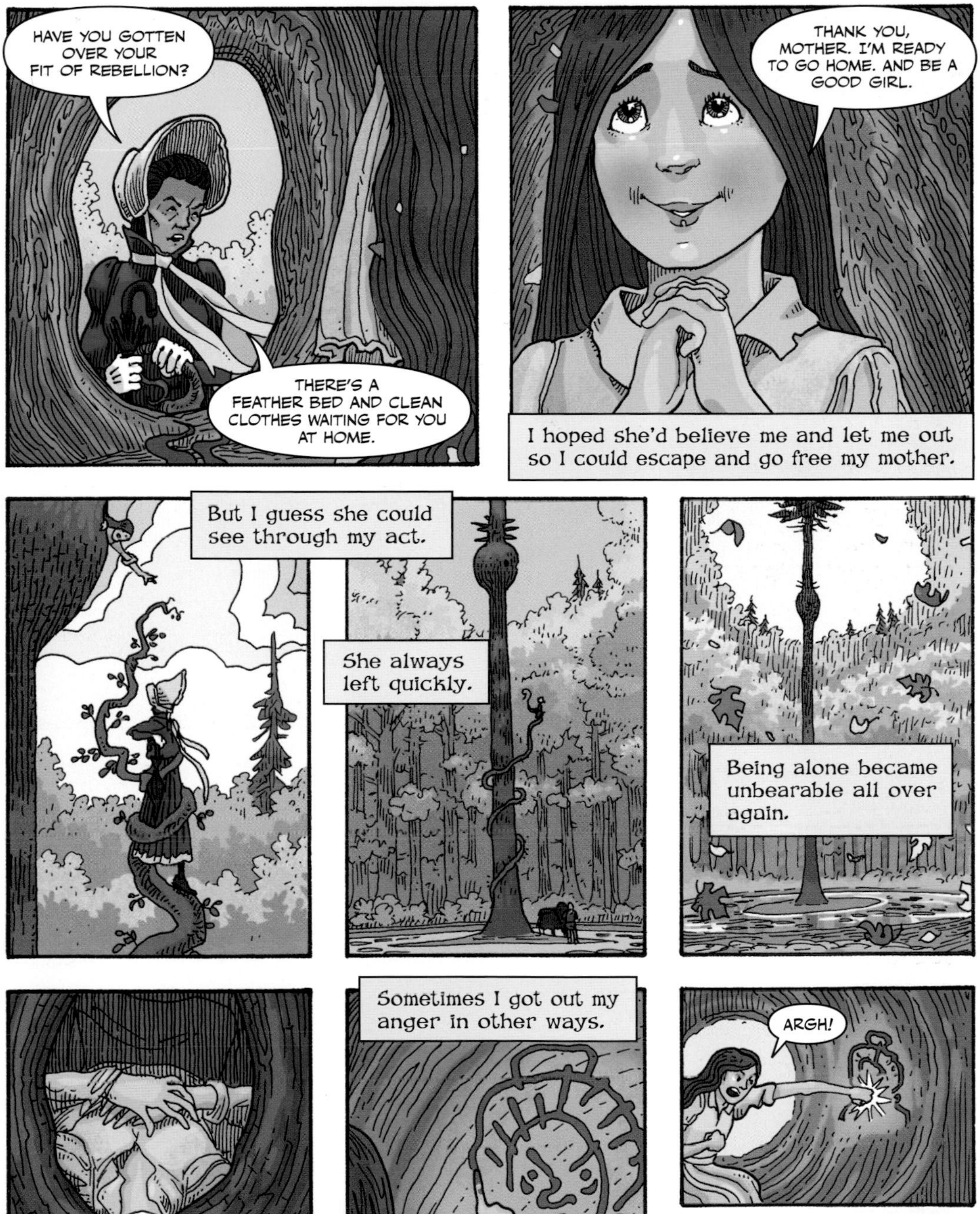
HAVE YOU GOTTEN OVER YOUR FIT OF REBELLION?
THERE'S A FEATHER BED AND CLEAN CLOTHES WAITING FOR YOU AT HOME.
THANK YOU, MOTHER. I'M READY TO GO HOME. AND BE A GOOD GIRL.
I hoped she'd believe me and let me out so I could escape and go free my mother.
But I guess she could see through my act.
She always left quickly.
Being alone became unbearable all over again.
Sometimes I cried myself silly.
Sometimes I got out my anger in other ways.
ARGH!
OW.

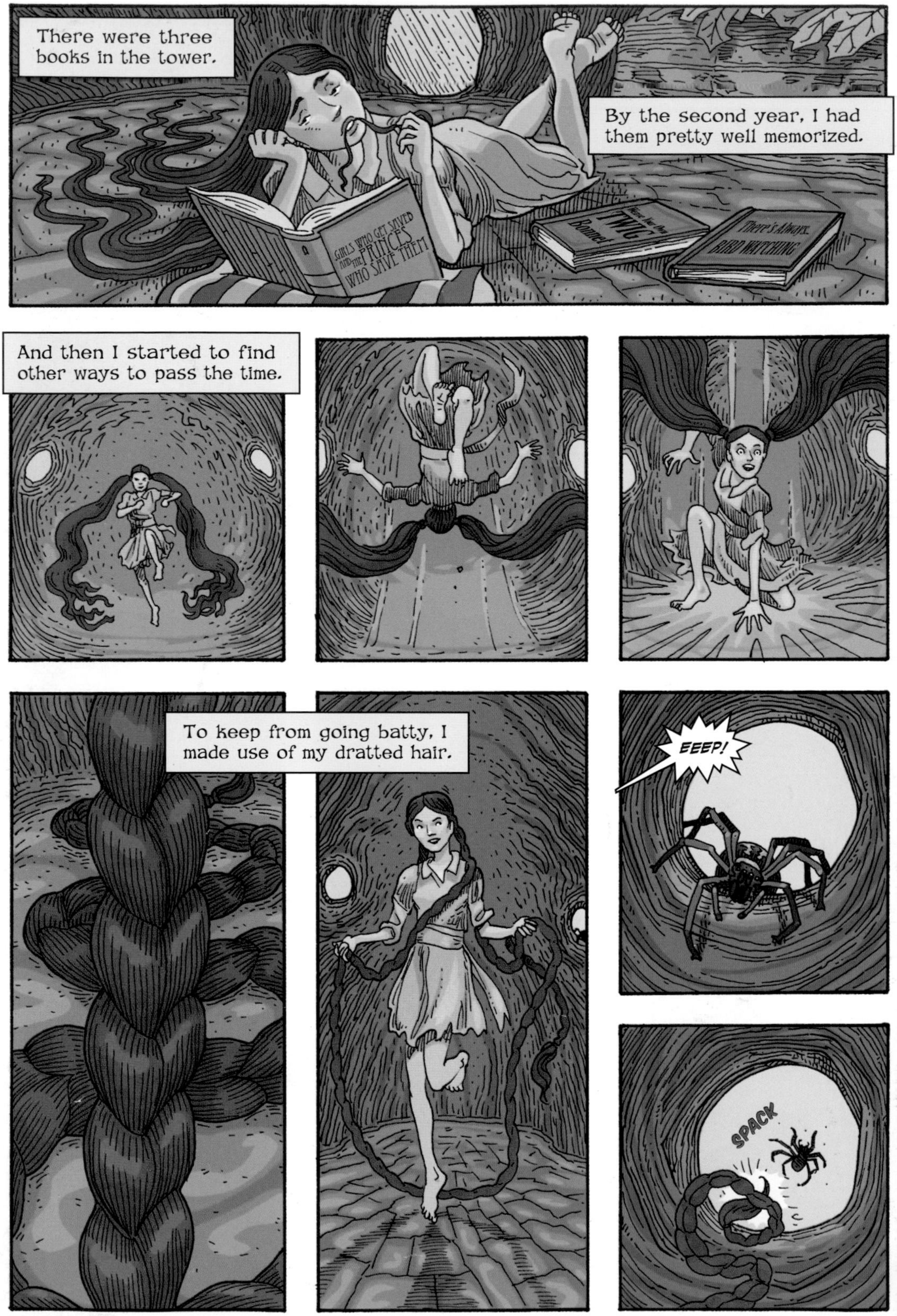
There were three books in the tower.
By the second year, I had them pretty well memorized.
GIRLS WHO GET SAVED AND THE PRINCES WHO SAVE THEM
Weave Your Own TWIG Bonnet
There's Always BIRD WATCHING
And then I started to find other ways to pass the time.
To keep from going batty, I made use of my dratted hair.
EEEP!
SPACK

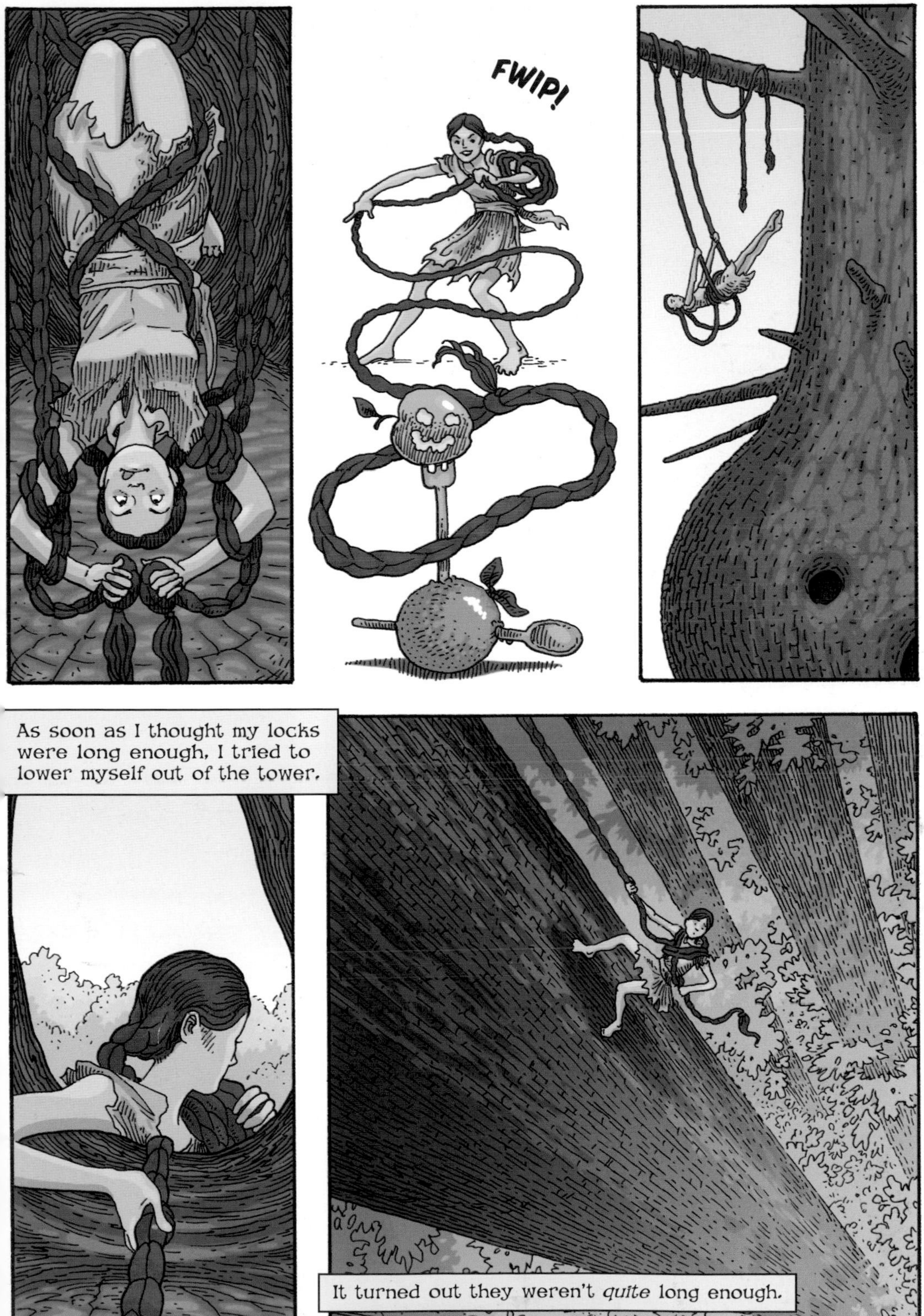
FWIP!
As soon as I thought my locks were long enough, I tried to lower myself out of the tower.
It turned out they weren't *quite* long enough.

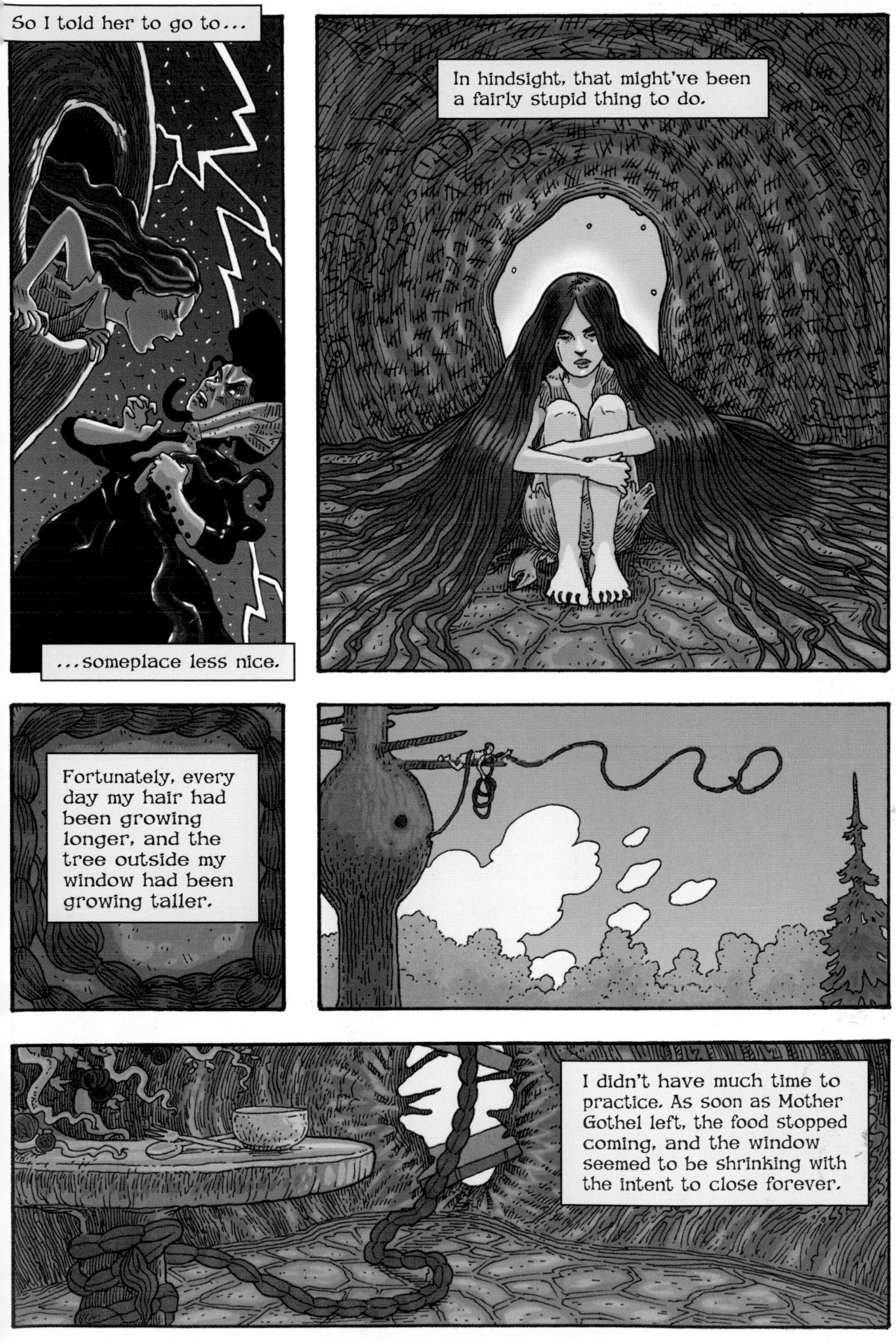
So I told her to go to...
...someplace less nice.
In hindsight, that might've been a fairly stupid thing to do.
Fortunately, every day my hair had been growing longer, and the tree outside my window had been growing taller.
I didn't have much time to practice. As soon as Mother Gothel left, the food stopped coming, and the window seemed to be shrinking with the intent to close forever.

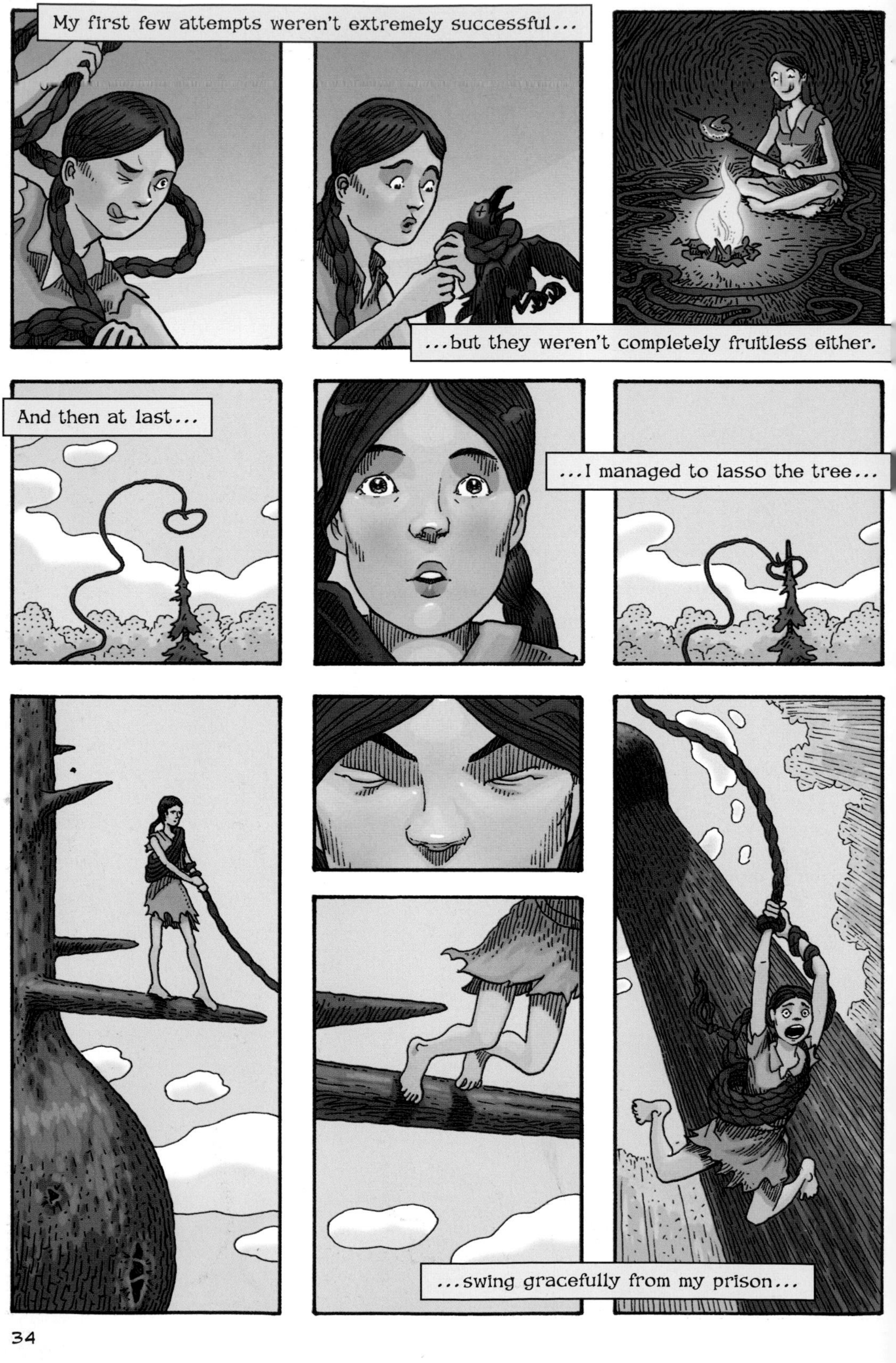

My first few attempts weren't extremely successful...
...but they weren't completely fruitless either.
And then at last...
...I managed to lasso the tree...
...swing gracefully from my prison...

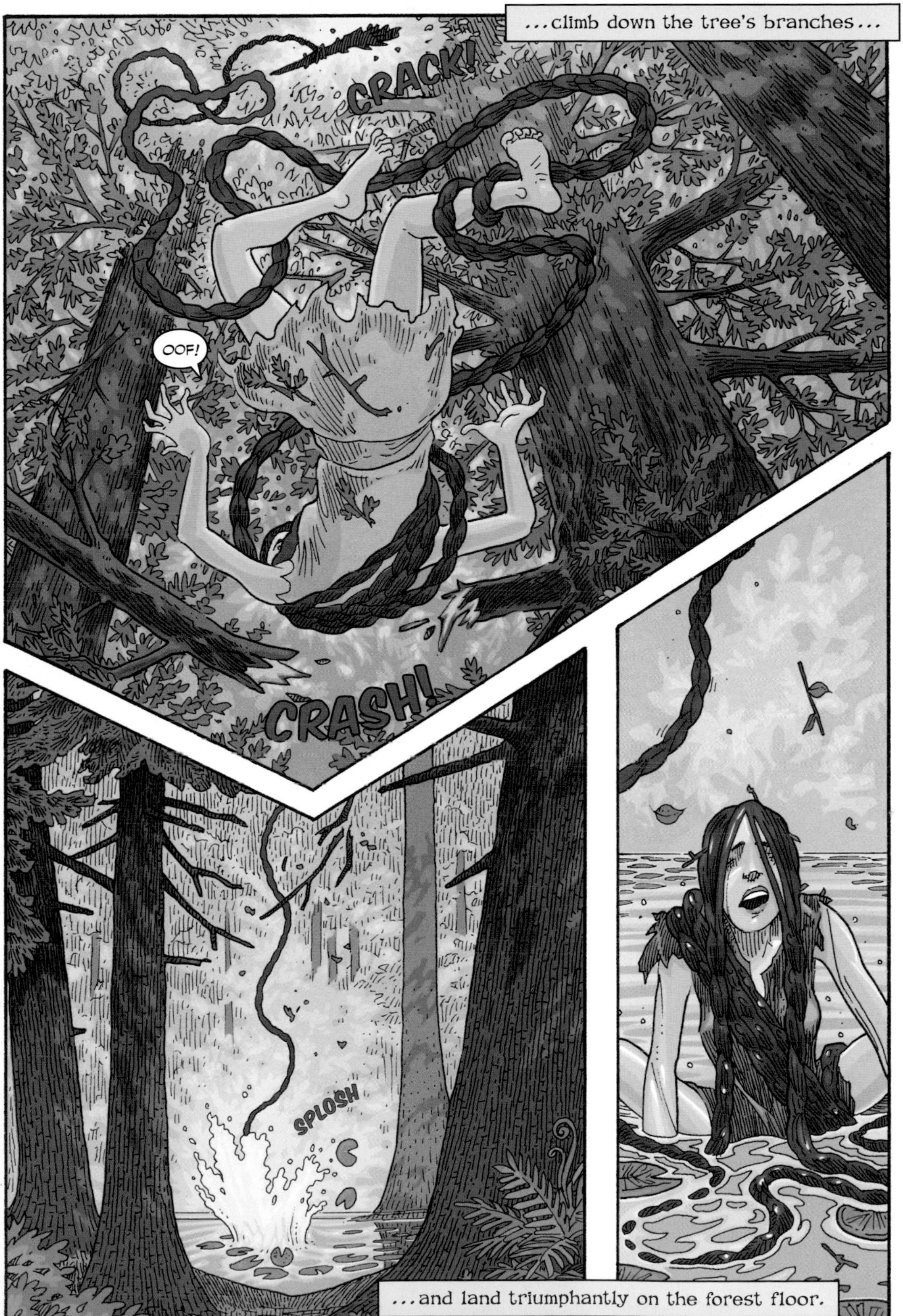
...climb down the tree's branches...
CRACK!
OOF!
CRASH!
SPLOSH
...and land triumphantly on the forest floor.

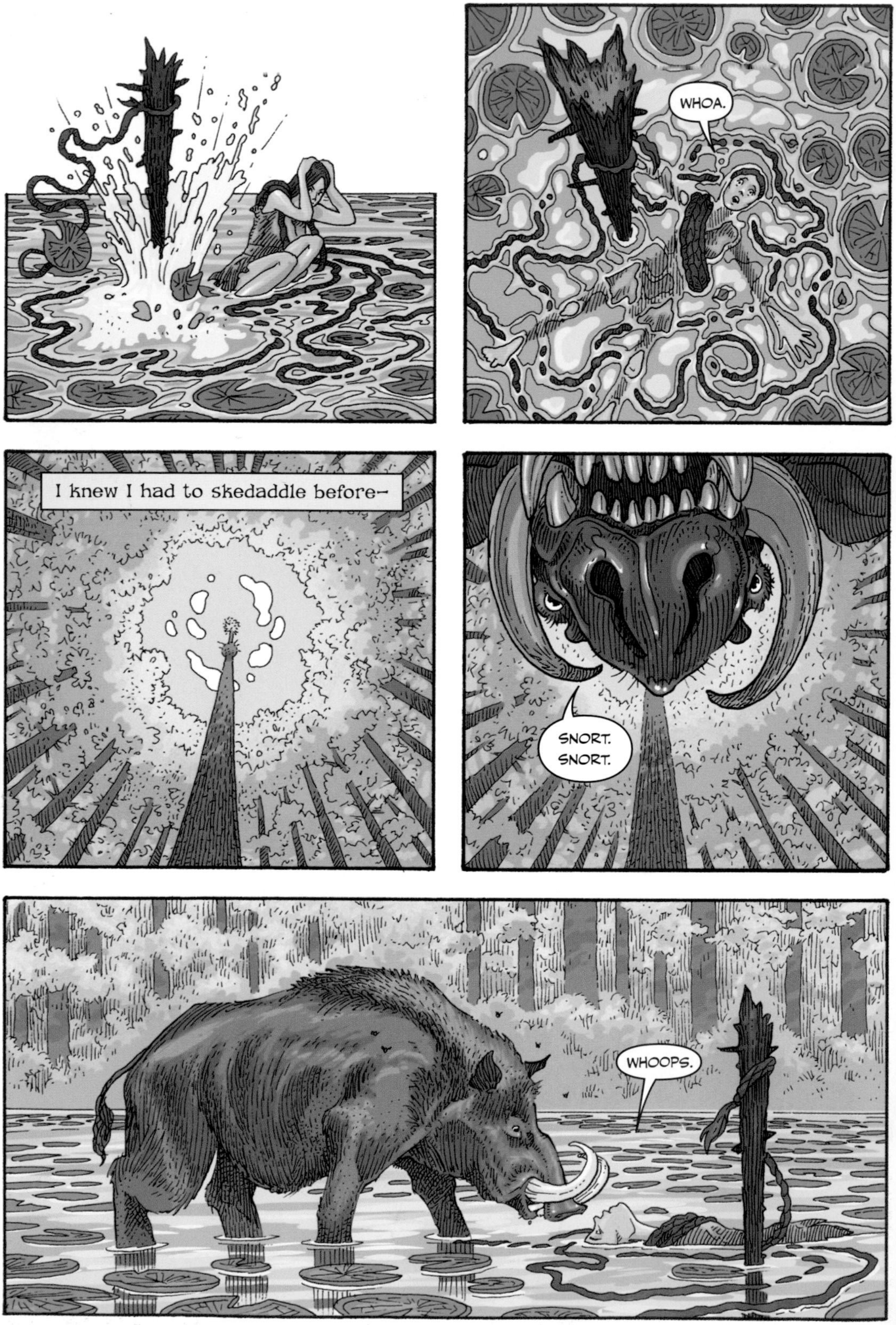
WHOA.
I knew I had to skedaddle before—
SNORT.
SNORT.
WHOOPS.

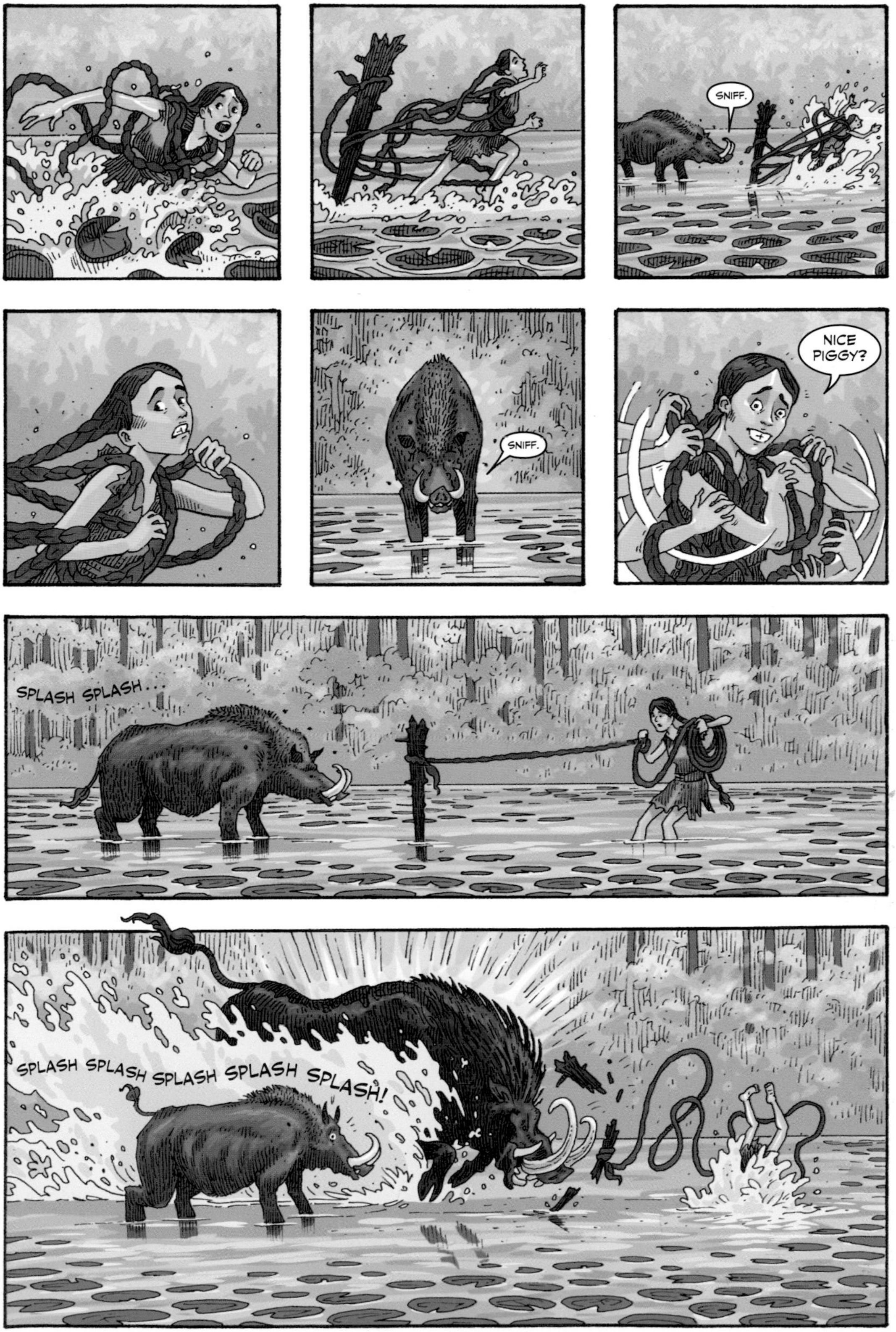
SNIFF.
SNIFF.
NICE PIGGY?
SPLASH SPLASH...
SPLASH SPLASH SPLASH SPLASH SPLASH!

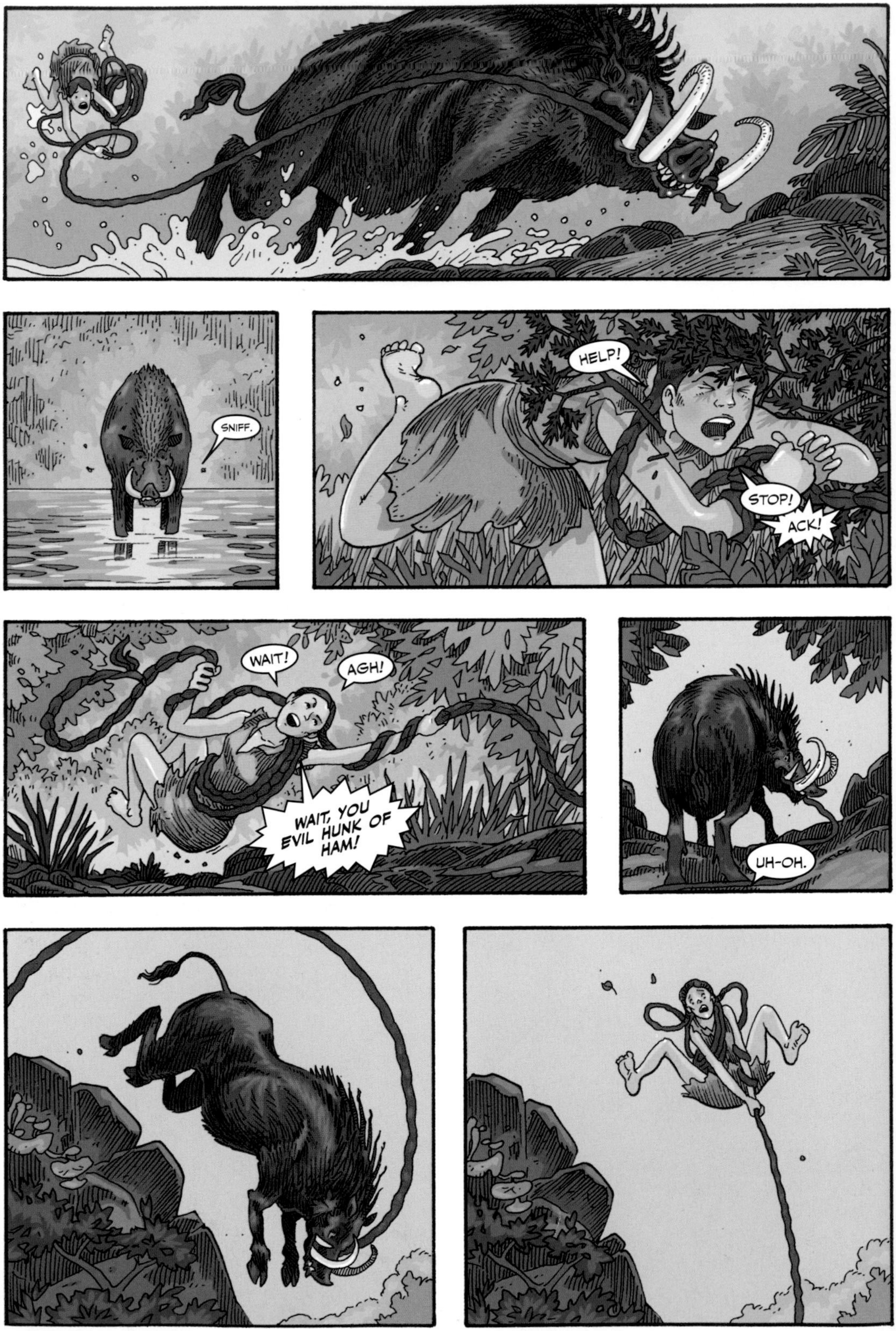
SNIFF.
HELP!
STOP!
ACK!
WAIT!
AGH!
WAIT, YOU EVIL HUNK OF HAM!
UH-OH.

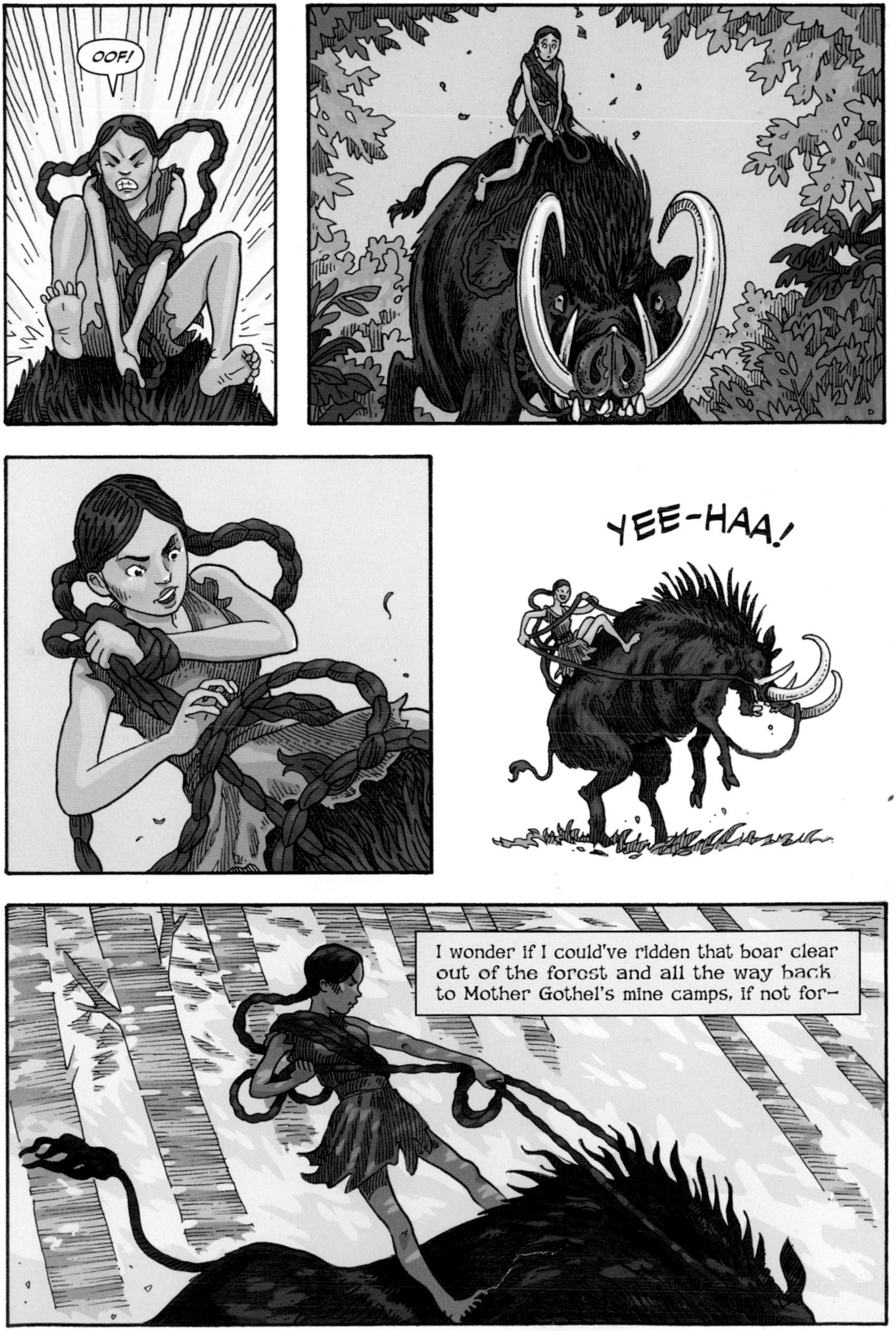

OOF!
YEE-HAA!
I wonder if I could've ridden that boar clear out of the forest and all the way back to Mother Gothel's mine camps, if not for–

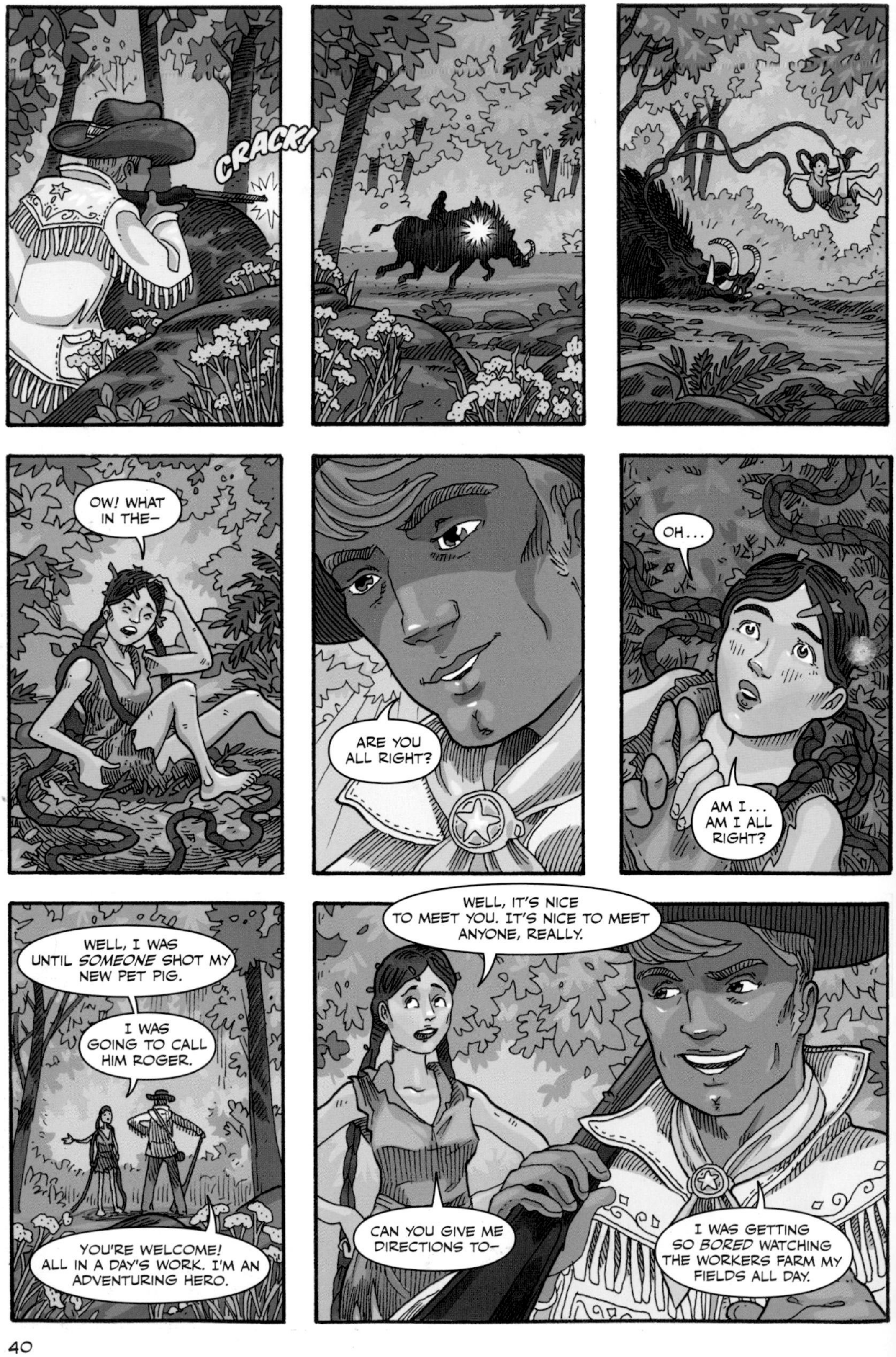
CRACK!
OW! WHAT IN THE–
ARE YOU ALL RIGHT?
OH...
AM I... AM I ALL RIGHT?
WELL, I WAS UNTIL *SOMEONE* SHOT MY NEW PET PIG.
I WAS GOING TO CALL HIM ROGER.
YOU'RE WELCOME! ALL IN A DAY'S WORK. I'M AN ADVENTURING HERO.
WELL, IT'S NICE TO MEET YOU. IT'S NICE TO MEET ANYONE, REALLY.
CAN YOU GIVE ME DIRECTIONS TO–
I WAS GETTING SO *BORED* WATCHING THE WORKERS FARM MY FIELDS ALL DAY.

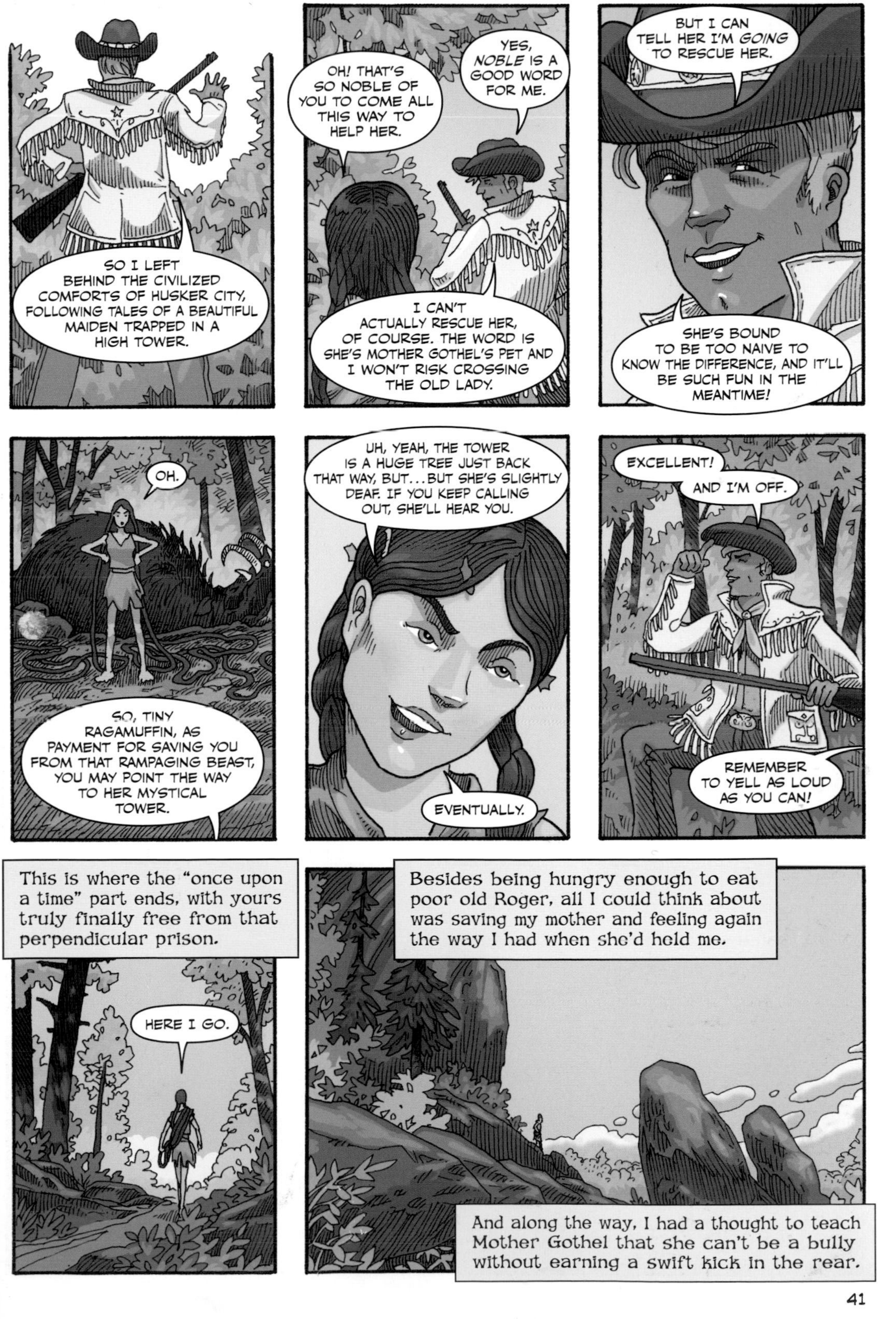
SO I LEFT BEHIND THE CIVILIZED COMFORTS OF HUSKER CITY, FOLLOWING TALES OF A BEAUTIFUL MAIDEN TRAPPED IN A HIGH TOWER.
OH! THAT'S SO NOBLE OF YOU TO COME ALL THIS WAY TO HELP HER.
YES, NOBLE IS A GOOD WORD FOR ME.
I CAN'T ACTUALLY RESCUE HER, OF COURSE. THE WORD IS SHE'S MOTHER GOTHEL'S PET AND I WON'T RISK CROSSING THE OLD LADY.
BUT I CAN TELL HER I'M GOING TO RESCUE HER.
SHE'S BOUND TO BE TOO NAIVE TO KNOW THE DIFFERENCE, AND IT'LL BE SUCH FUN IN THE MEANTIME!
OH.
SO, TINY RAGAMUFFIN, AS PAYMENT FOR SAVING YOU FROM THAT RAMPAGING BEAST, YOU MAY POINT THE WAY TO HER MYSTICAL TOWER.
UH, YEAH, THE TOWER IS A HUGE TREE JUST BACK THAT WAY, BUT... BUT SHE'S SLIGHTLY DEAF. IF YOU KEEP CALLING OUT, SHE'LL HEAR YOU.
EVENTUALLY.
EXCELLENT!
AND I'M OFF.
REMEMBER TO YELL AS LOUD AS YOU CAN!
This is where the "once upon a time" part ends, with yours truly finally free from that perpendicular prison.
HERE I GO.
Besides being hungry enough to eat poor old Roger, all I could think about was saving my mother and feeling again the way I had when she'd held me.
And along the way, I had a thought to teach Mother Gothel that she can't be a bully without earning a swift kick in the rear.

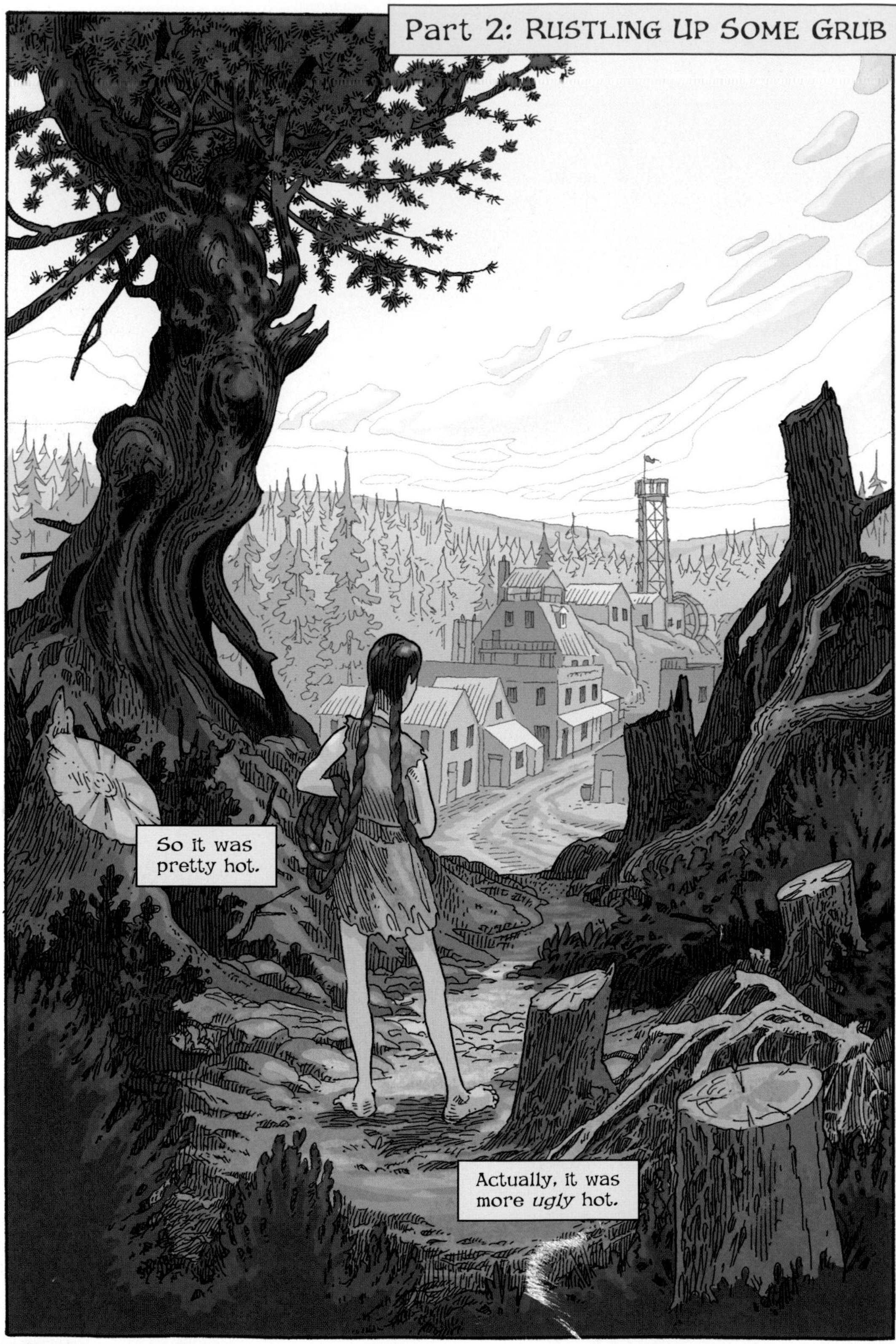
Part 2: Rustling Up Some Grub
So it was pretty hot.
Actually, it was more *ugly* hot.

44

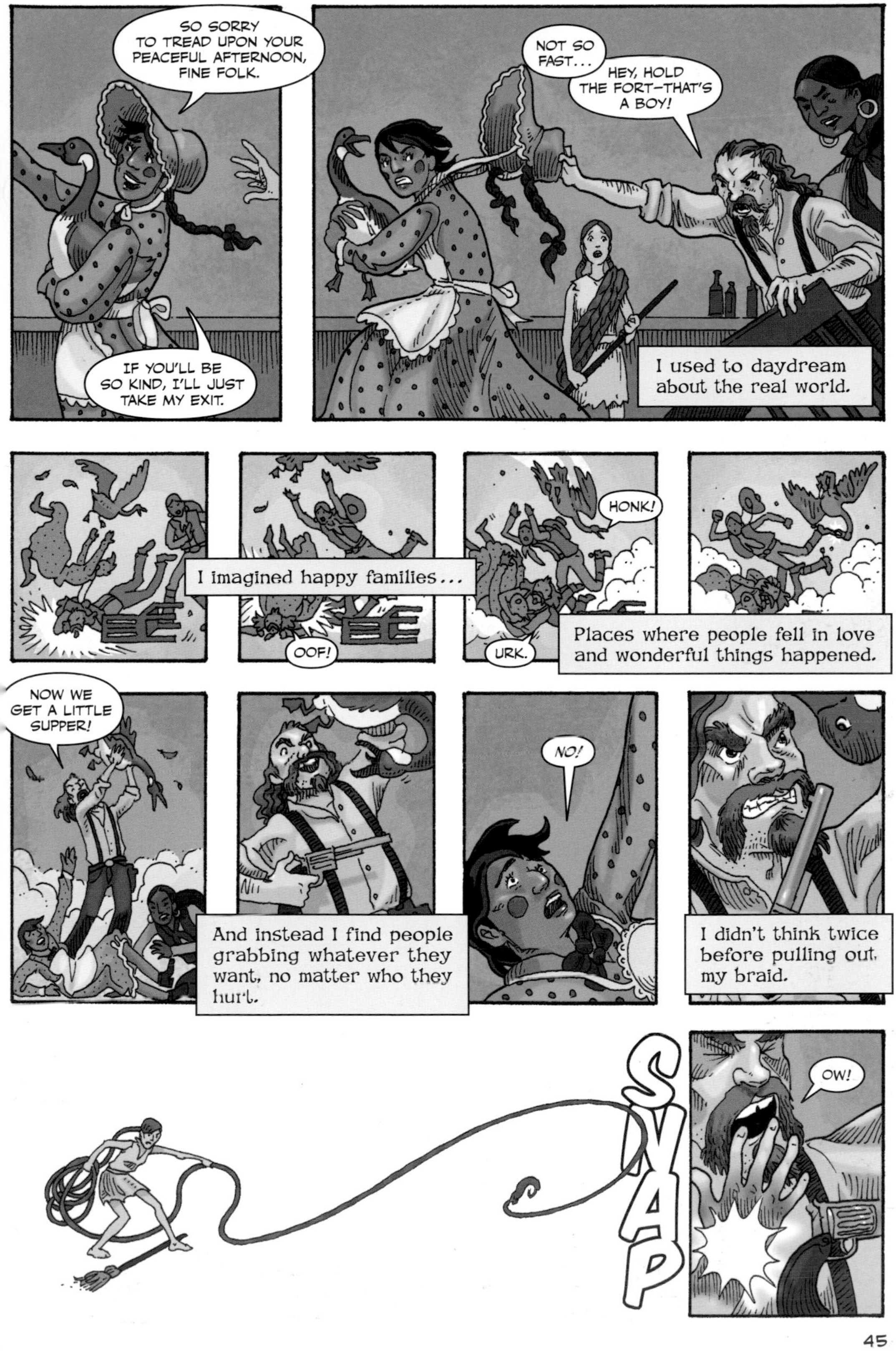
SO SORRY TO TREAD UPON YOUR PEACEFUL AFTERNOON, FINE FOLK.
IF YOU'LL BE SO KIND, I'LL JUST TAKE MY EXIT.
NOT SO FAST...
HEY, HOLD THE FORT—THAT'S A BOY!
I used to daydream about the real world.
I imagined happy families...
OOF!
HONK!
URK.
Places where people fell in love and wonderful things happened.
NOW WE GET A LITTLE SUPPER!
And instead I find people grabbing whatever they want, no matter who they hurt.
NO!
I didn't think twice before pulling out my braid.
SNAP
OW!

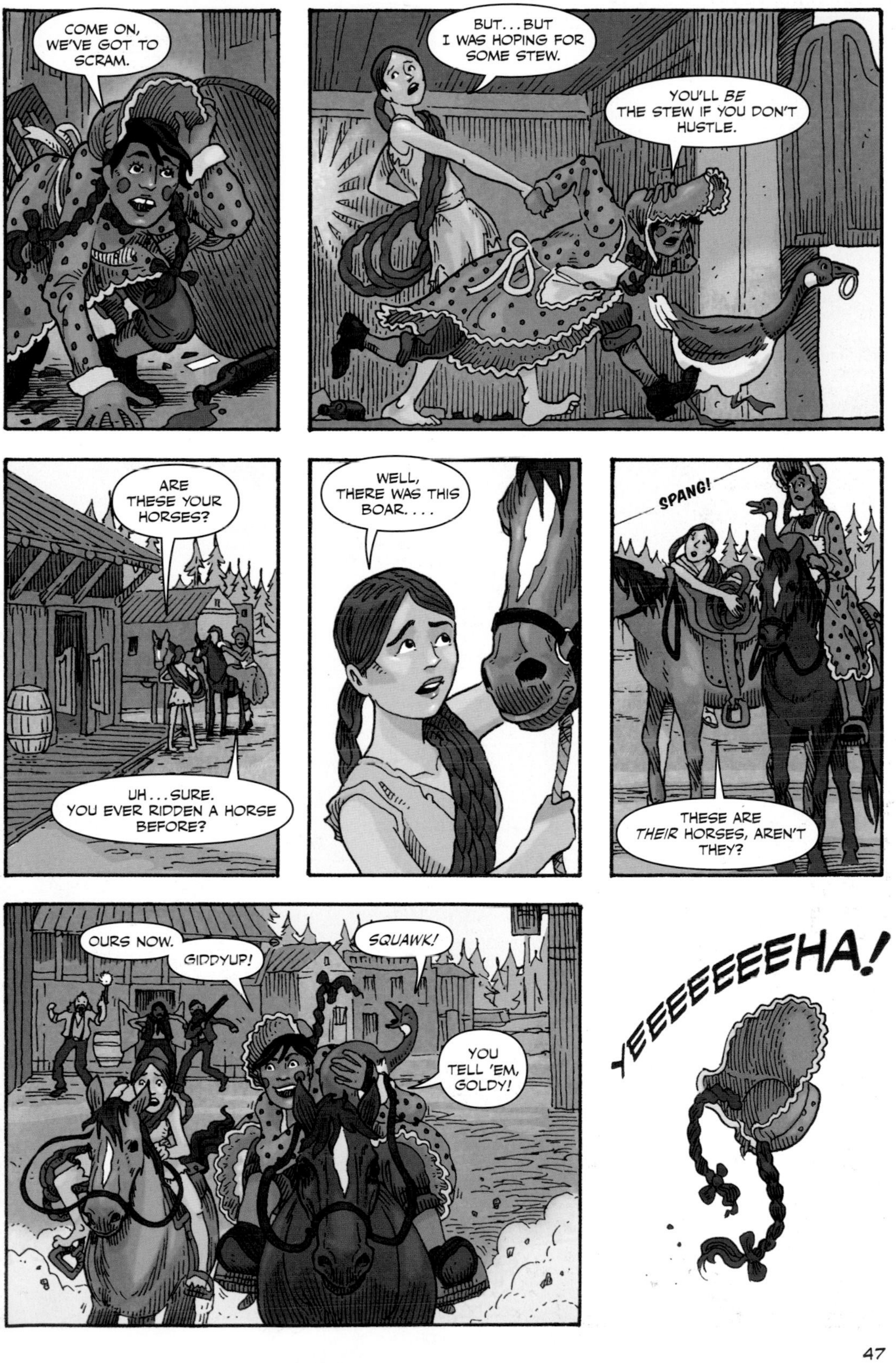
COME ON, WE'VE GOT TO SCRAM.
BUT...BUT I WAS HOPING FOR SOME STEW.
YOU'LL *BE* THE STEW IF YOU DON'T HUSTLE.
ARE THESE YOUR HORSES?
UH...SURE. YOU EVER RIDDEN A HORSE BEFORE?
WELL, THERE WAS THIS BOAR....
SPANG!
THESE ARE *THEIR* HORSES, AREN'T THEY?
OURS NOW.
GIDDYUP!
SQUAWK!
YOU TELL 'EM, GOLDY!
YEEEEEEEHA!

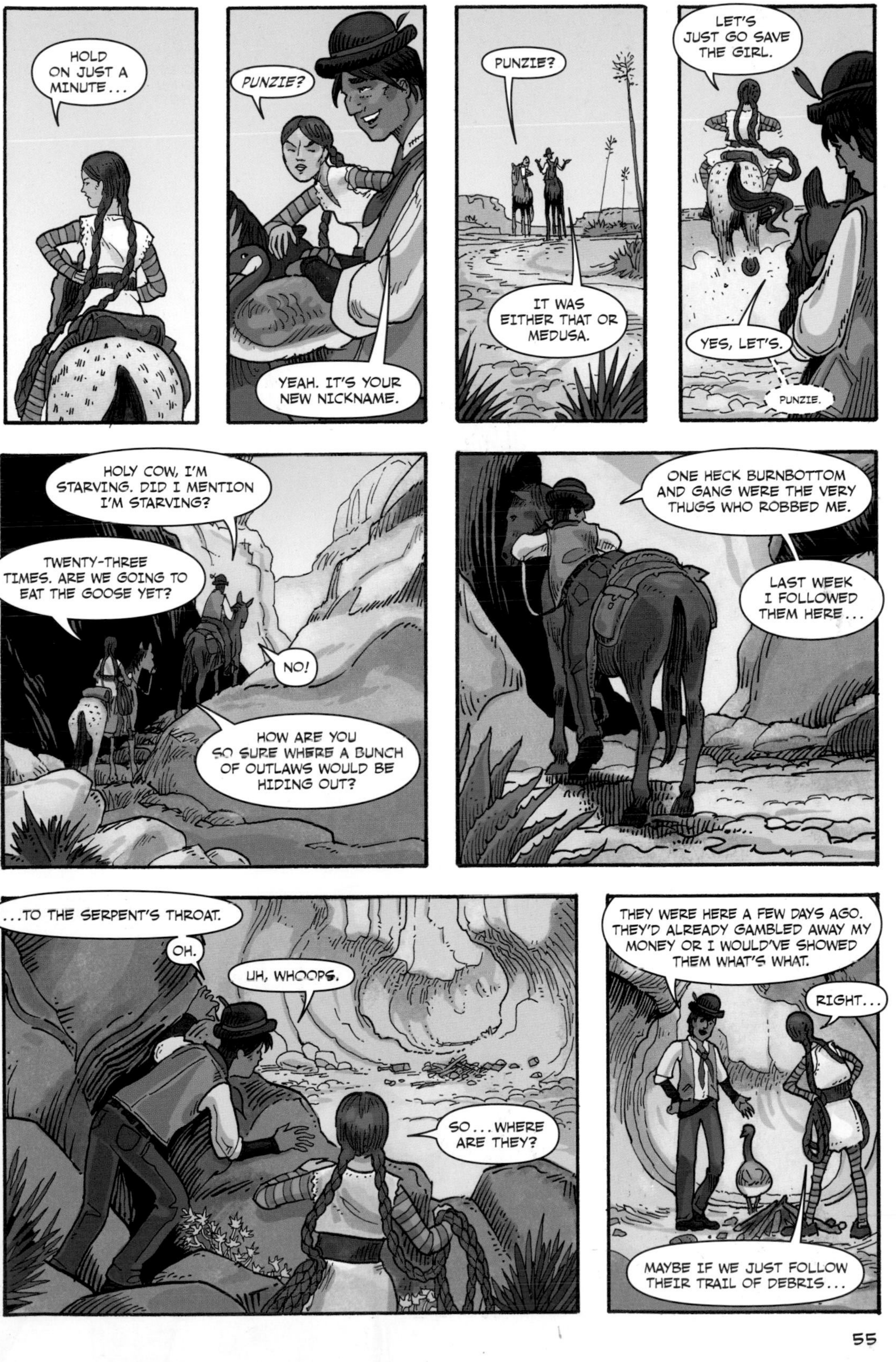
HOLD ON JUST A MINUTE...
PUNZIE?
YEAH. IT'S YOUR NEW NICKNAME.
PUNZIE?
IT WAS EITHER THAT OR MEDUSA.
LET'S JUST GO SAVE THE GIRL.
YES, LET'S.
PUNZIE.
HOLY COW, I'M STARVING. DID I MENTION I'M STARVING?
TWENTY-THREE TIMES. ARE WE GOING TO EAT THE GOOSE YET?
NO!
HOW ARE YOU SO SURE WHERE A BUNCH OF OUTLAWS WOULD BE HIDING OUT?
ONE HECK BURNBOTTOM AND GANG WERE THE VERY THUGS WHO ROBBED ME.
LAST WEEK I FOLLOWED THEM HERE...
...TO THE SERPENT'S THROAT.
OH.
UH, WHOOPS.
SO...WHERE ARE THEY?
THEY WERE HERE A FEW DAYS AGO. THEY'D ALREADY GAMBLED AWAY MY MONEY OR I WOULD'VE SHOWED THEM WHAT'S WHAT.
RIGHT...
MAYBE IF WE JUST FOLLOW THEIR TRAIL OF DEBRIS...

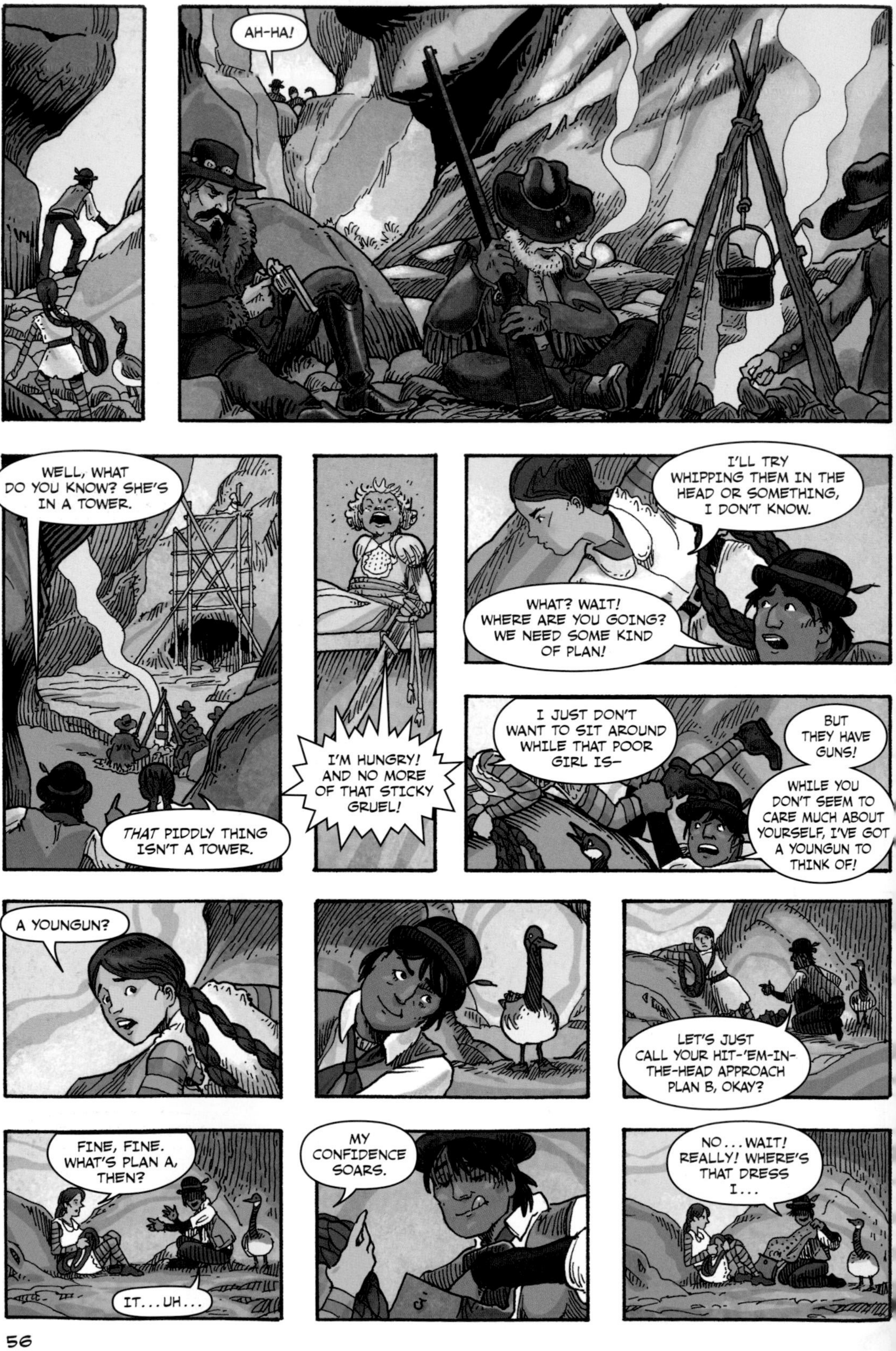
AH-HA!
WELL, WHAT DO YOU KNOW? SHE'S IN A TOWER.
THAT PIDDLY THING ISN'T A TOWER.
I'M HUNGRY! AND NO MORE OF THAT STICKY GRUEL!
I'LL TRY WHIPPING THEM IN THE HEAD OR SOMETHING, I DON'T KNOW.
WHAT? WAIT! WHERE ARE YOU GOING? WE NEED SOME KIND OF PLAN!
I JUST DON'T WANT TO SIT AROUND WHILE THAT POOR GIRL IS-
BUT THEY HAVE GUNS!
WHILE YOU DON'T SEEM TO CARE MUCH ABOUT YOURSELF, I'VE GOT A YOUNGUN TO THINK OF!
A YOUNGUN?
LET'S JUST CALL YOUR HIT-'EM-IN-THE-HEAD APPROACH PLAN B, OKAY?
FINE, FINE. WHAT'S PLAN A, THEN?
IT... UH...
MY CONFIDENCE SOARS.
NO... WAIT! REALLY! WHERE'S THAT DRESS I...

58

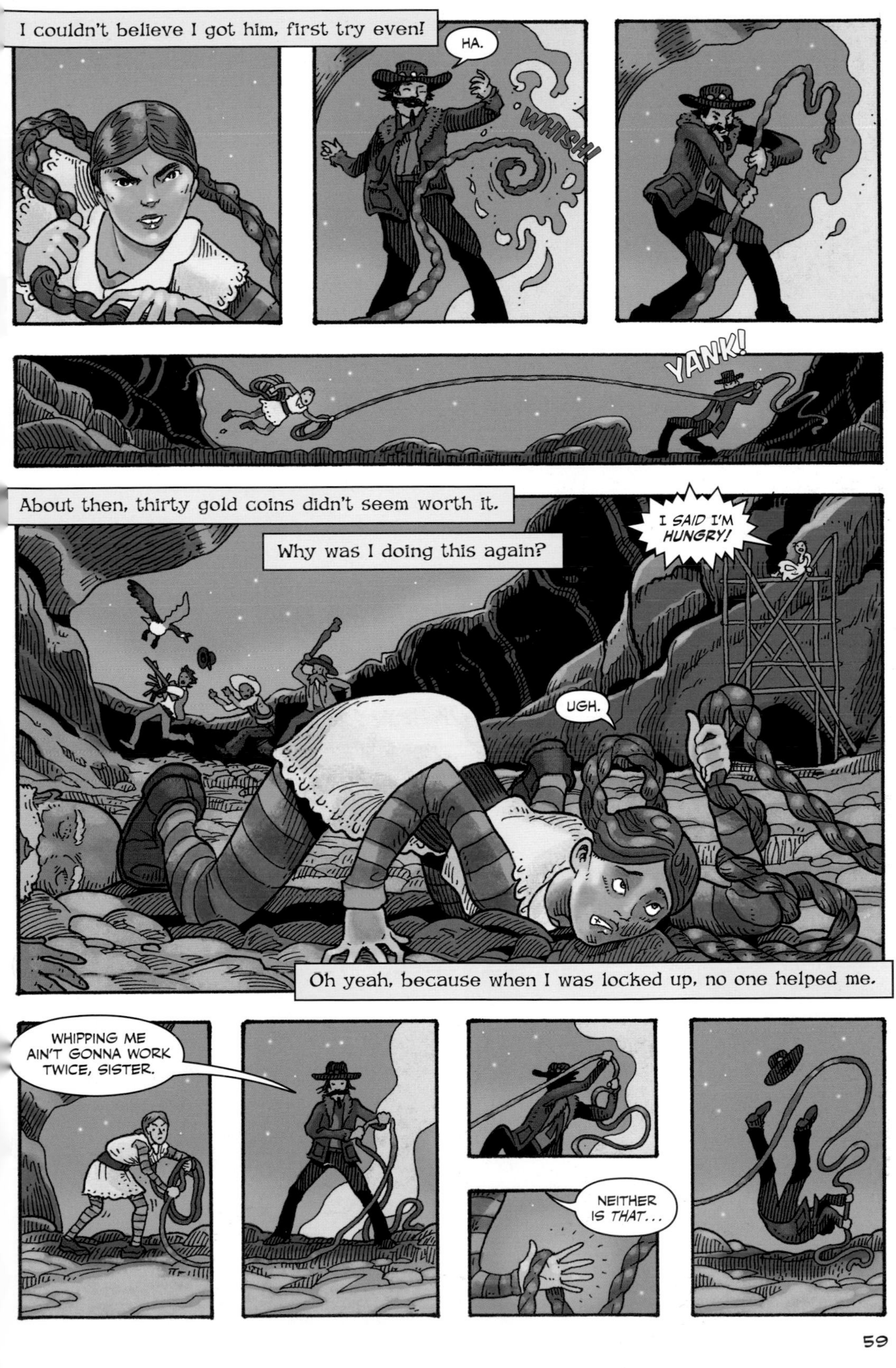

I couldn't believe I got him, first try even!
HA.
WHISH!
YANK!
About then, thirty gold coins didn't seem worth it.
Why was I doing this again?
I SAID I'M HUNGRY!
UGH.
Oh yeah, because when I was locked up, no one helped me.
WHIPPING ME AIN'T GONNA WORK TWICE, SISTER.
NEITHER IS THAT...

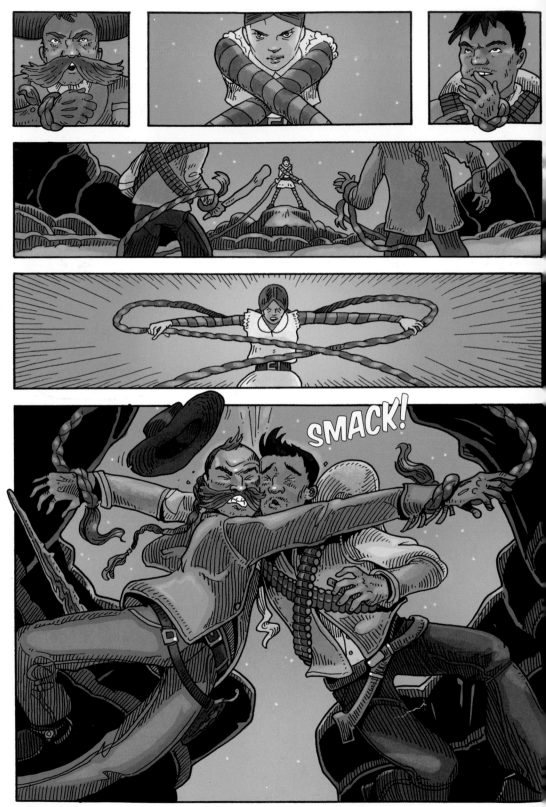

SMACK!

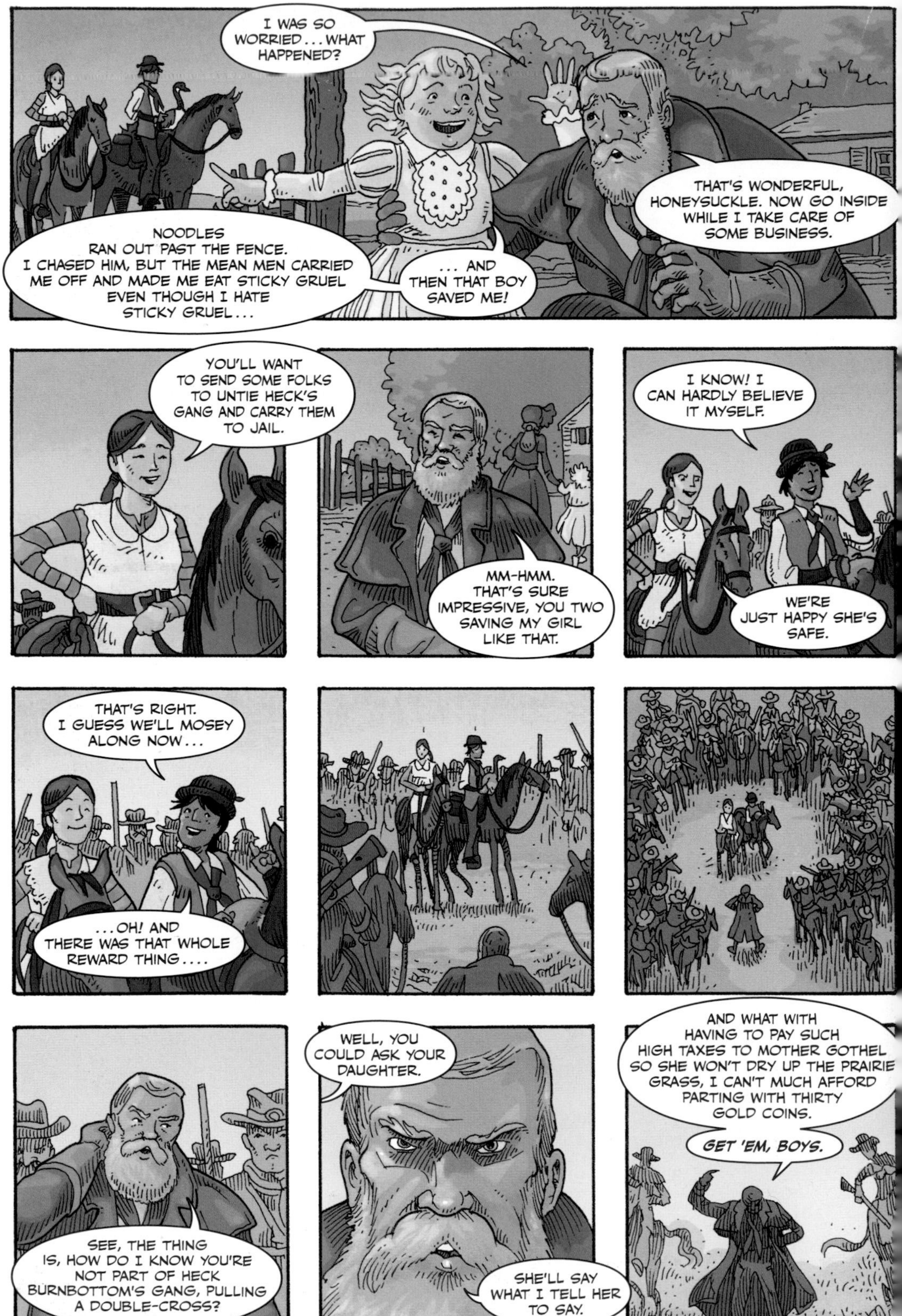
I WAS SO WORRIED . . . WHAT HAPPENED?
NOODLES RAN OUT PAST THE FENCE. I CHASED HIM, BUT THE MEAN MEN CARRIED ME OFF AND MADE ME EAT STICKY GRUEL EVEN THOUGH I HATE STICKY GRUEL . . .
. . . AND THEN THAT BOY SAVED ME!
THAT'S WONDERFUL, HONEYSUCKLE. NOW GO INSIDE WHILE I TAKE CARE OF SOME BUSINESS.
YOU'LL WANT TO SEND SOME FOLKS TO UNTIE HECK'S GANG AND CARRY THEM TO JAIL.
MM-HMM. THAT'S SURE IMPRESSIVE, YOU TWO SAVING MY GIRL LIKE THAT.
I KNOW! I CAN HARDLY BELIEVE IT MYSELF.
WE'RE JUST HAPPY SHE'S SAFE.
THAT'S RIGHT. I GUESS WE'LL MOSEY ALONG NOW . . .
. . . OH! AND THERE WAS THAT WHOLE REWARD THING . . . .
SEE, THE THING IS, HOW DO I KNOW YOU'RE NOT PART OF HECK BURNBOTTOM'S GANG, PULLING A DOUBLE-CROSS?
WELL, YOU COULD ASK YOUR DAUGHTER.
SHE'LL SAY WHAT I TELL HER TO SAY.
AND WHAT WITH HAVING TO PAY SUCH HIGH TAXES TO MOTHER GOTHEL SO SHE WON'T DRY UP THE PRAIRIE GRASS, I CAN'T MUCH AFFORD PARTING WITH THIRTY GOLD COINS.
GET 'EM, BOYS.

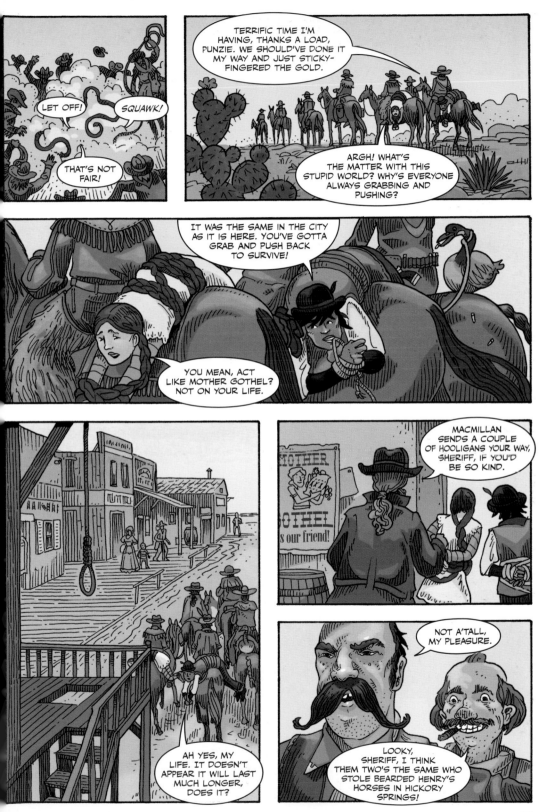

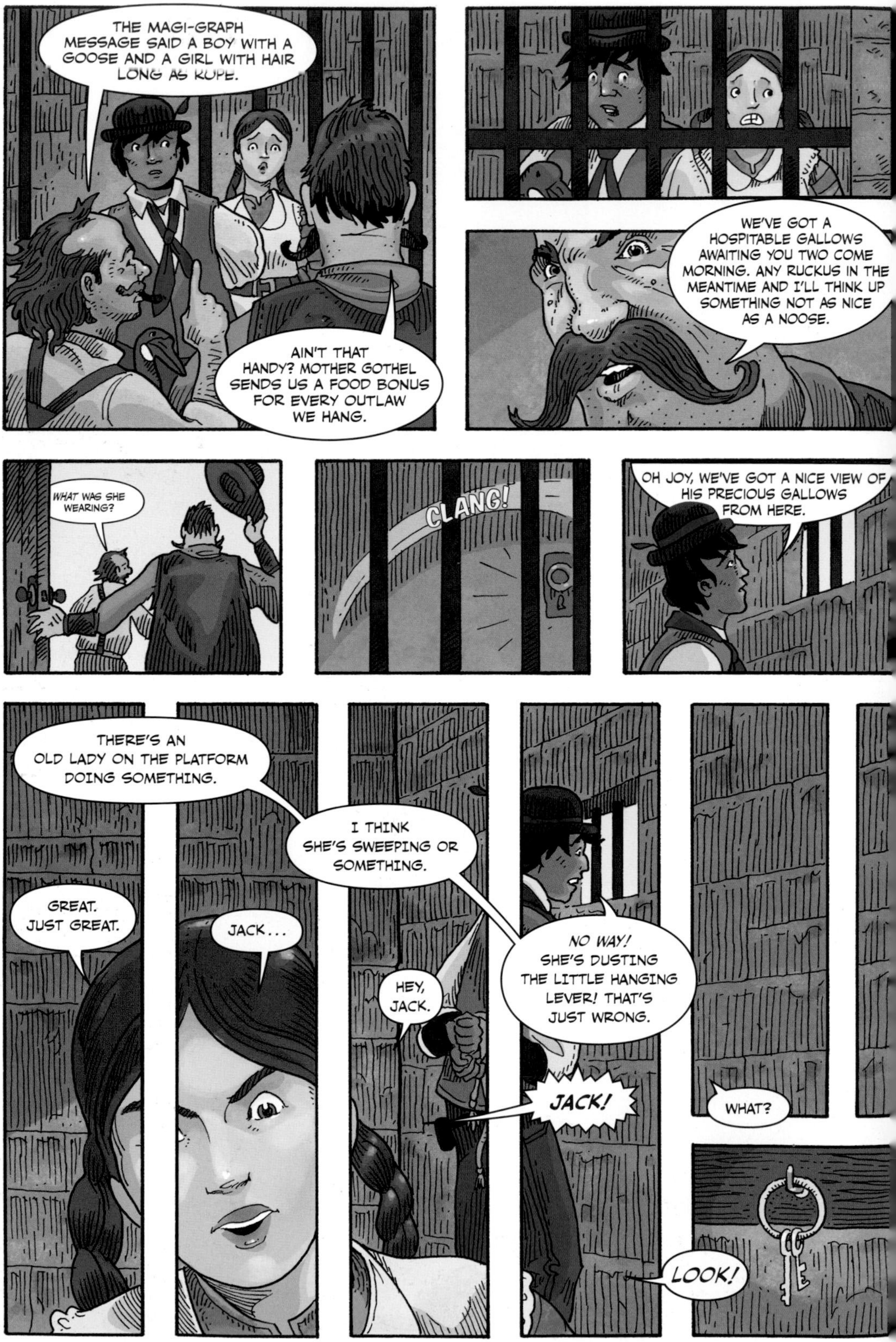
THE MAGI-GRAPH MESSAGE SAID A BOY WITH A GOOSE AND A GIRL WITH HAIR LONG AS ROPE.
AIN'T THAT HANDY? MOTHER GOTHEL SENDS US A FOOD BONUS FOR EVERY OUTLAW WE HANG.
WE'VE GOT A HOSPITABLE GALLOWS AWAITING YOU TWO COME MORNING. ANY RUCKUS IN THE MEANTIME AND I'LL THINK UP SOMETHING NOT AS NICE AS A NOOSE.
WHAT WAS SHE WEARING?
CLANG!
OH JOY, WE'VE GOT A NICE VIEW OF HIS PRECIOUS GALLOWS FROM HERE.
THERE'S AN OLD LADY ON THE PLATFORM DOING SOMETHING.
I THINK SHE'S SWEEPING OR SOMETHING.
GREAT. JUST GREAT.
JACK...
HEY, JACK.
NO WAY! SHE'S DUSTING THE LITTLE HANGING LEVER! THAT'S JUST WRONG.
JACK!
WHAT?
LOOK!

67

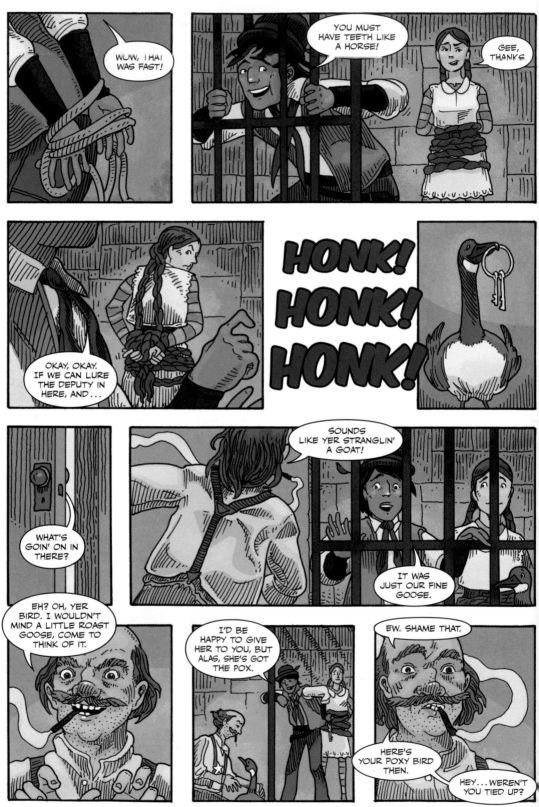

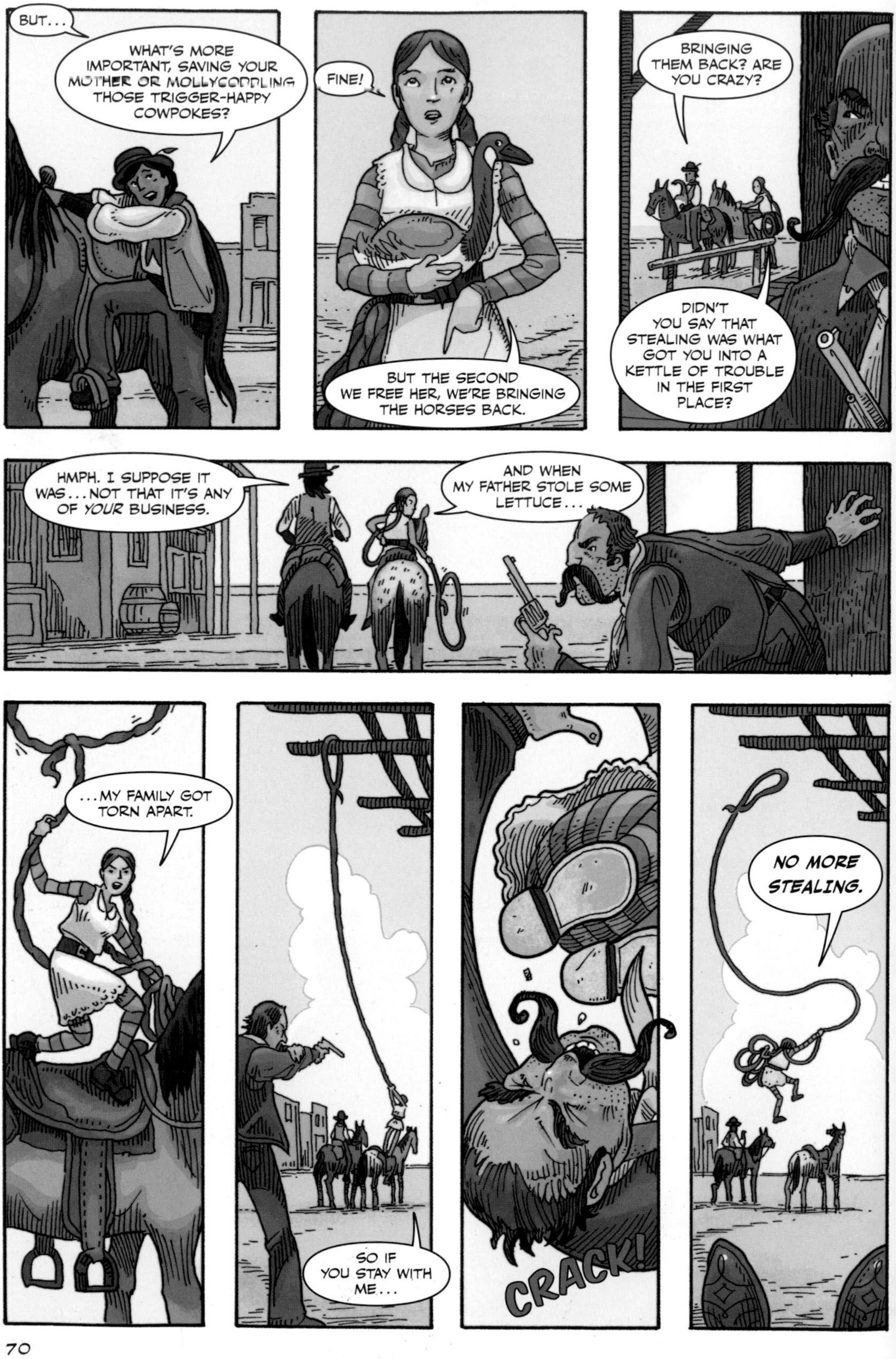

BUT...
WHAT'S MORE IMPORTANT, SAVING YOUR MOTHER OR MOLLYCODDLING THOSE TRIGGER-HAPPY COWPOKES?
FINE!
BUT THE SECOND WE FREE HER, WE'RE BRINGING THE HORSES BACK.
BRINGING THEM BACK? ARE YOU CRAZY?
DIDN'T YOU SAY THAT STEALING WAS WHAT GOT YOU INTO A KETTLE OF TROUBLE IN THE FIRST PLACE?
HMPH. I SUPPOSE IT WAS...NOT THAT IT'S ANY OF *YOUR* BUSINESS.
AND WHEN MY FATHER STOLE SOME LETTUCE...
...MY FAMILY GOT TORN APART.
SO IF YOU STAY WITH ME...
CRACK!
NO MORE STEALING.

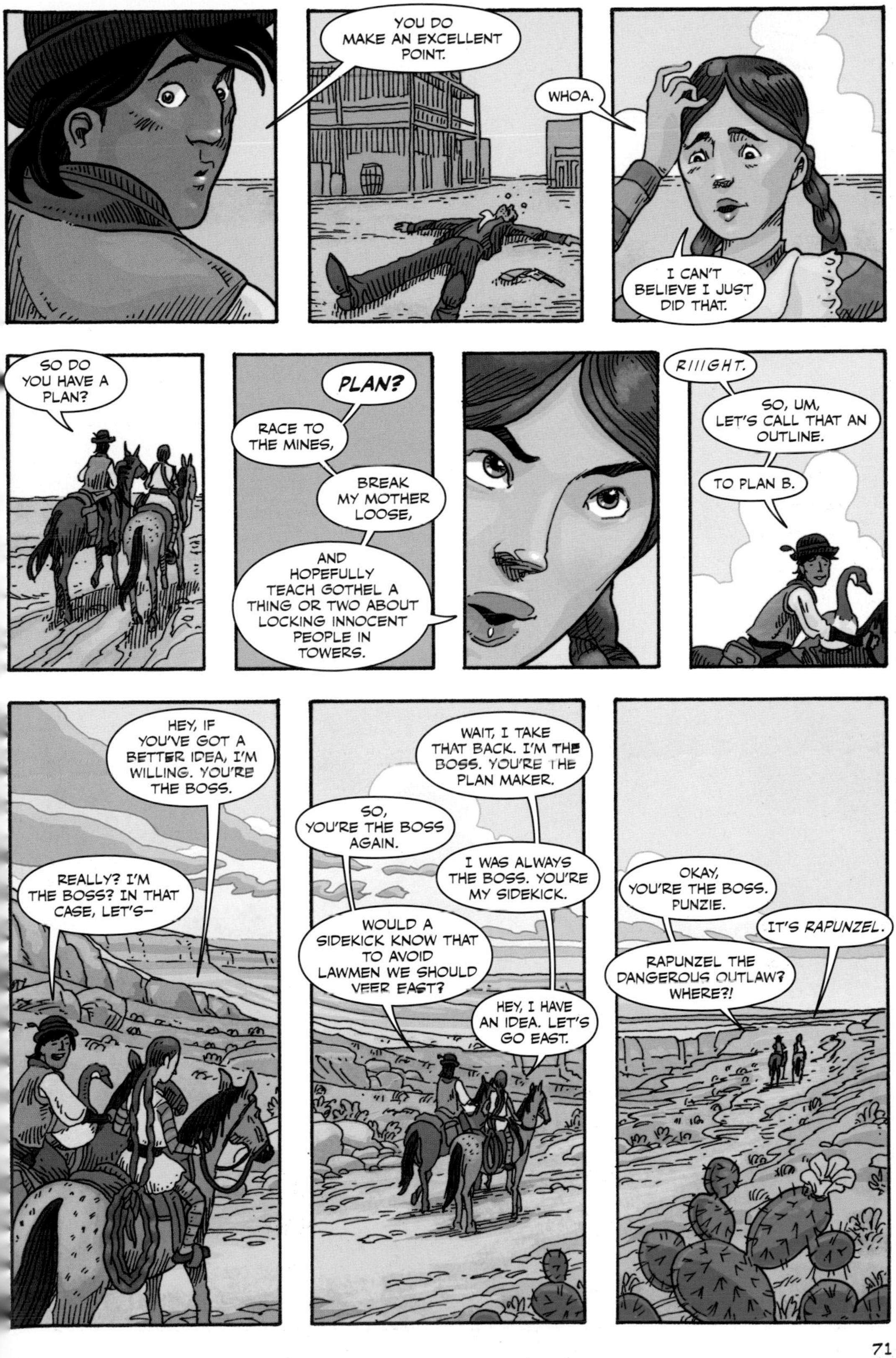
YOU DO MAKE AN EXCELLENT POINT.
WHOA.
I CAN'T BELIEVE I JUST DID THAT.
SO DO YOU HAVE A PLAN?
PLAN?
RACE TO THE MINES,
BREAK MY MOTHER LOOSE,
AND HOPEFULLY TEACH GOTHEL A THING OR TWO ABOUT LOCKING INNOCENT PEOPLE IN TOWERS.
RIIIGHT.
SO, UM, LET'S CALL THAT AN OUTLINE.
TO PLAN B.
HEY, IF YOU'VE GOT A BETTER IDEA, I'M WILLING. YOU'RE THE BOSS.
REALLY? I'M THE BOSS? IN THAT CASE, LET'S—
WAIT, I TAKE THAT BACK. I'M THE BOSS. YOU'RE THE PLAN MAKER.
SO, YOU'RE THE BOSS AGAIN.
I WAS ALWAYS THE BOSS. YOU'RE MY SIDEKICK.
WOULD A SIDEKICK KNOW THAT TO AVOID LAWMEN WE SHOULD VEER EAST?
HEY, I HAVE AN IDEA. LET'S GO EAST.
OKAY, YOU'RE THE BOSS. PUNZIE.
IT'S RAPUNZEL.
RAPUNZEL THE DANGEROUS OUTLAW? WHERE?!

Part 3: Banditry in the Badlands

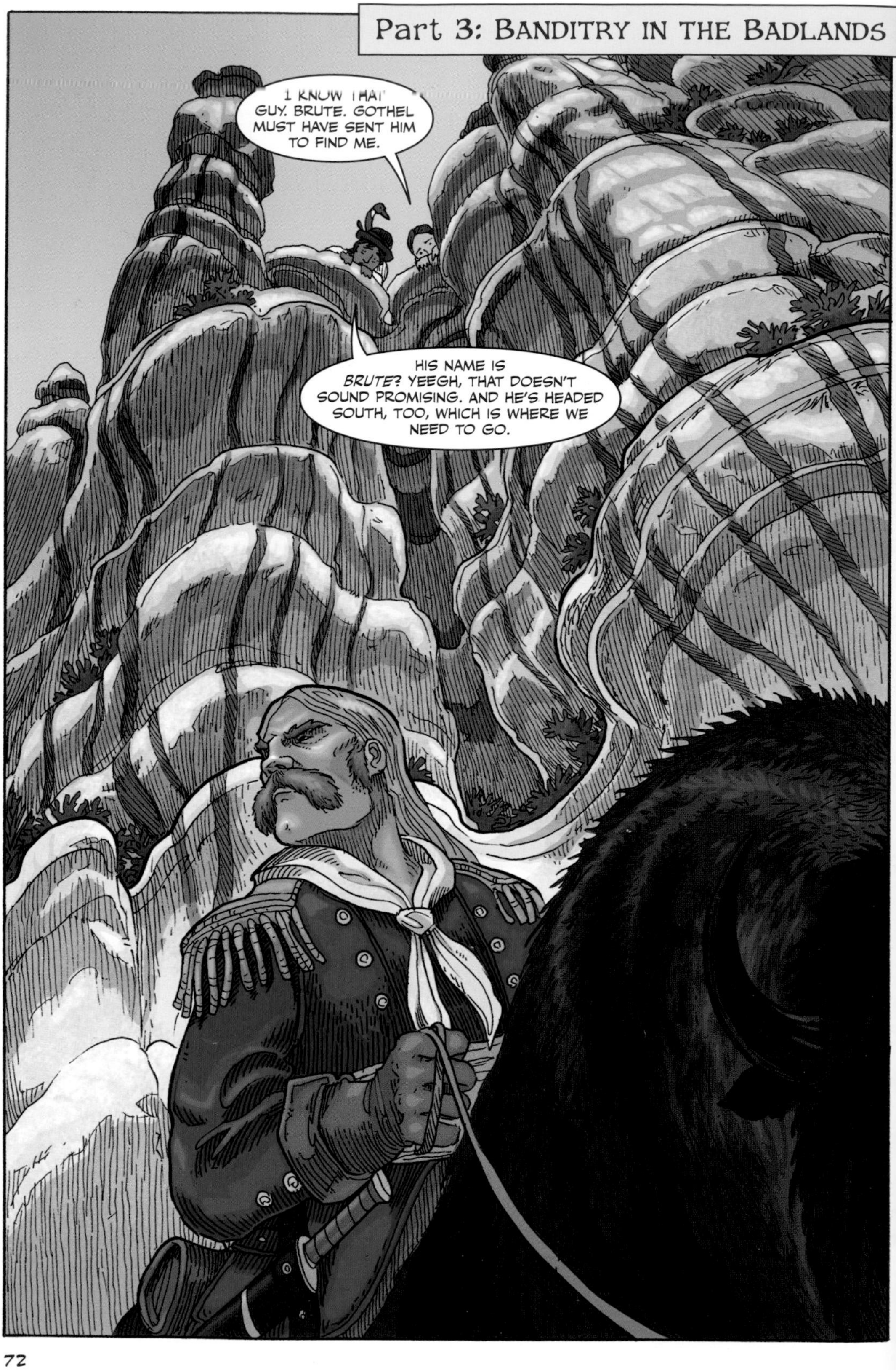
I KNOW THAT GUY. BRUTE. GOTHEL MUST HAVE SENT HIM TO FIND ME.
HIS NAME IS *BRUTE*? YEEGH, THAT DOESN'T SOUND PROMISING. AND HE'S HEADED SOUTH, TOO, WHICH IS WHERE WE NEED TO GO.

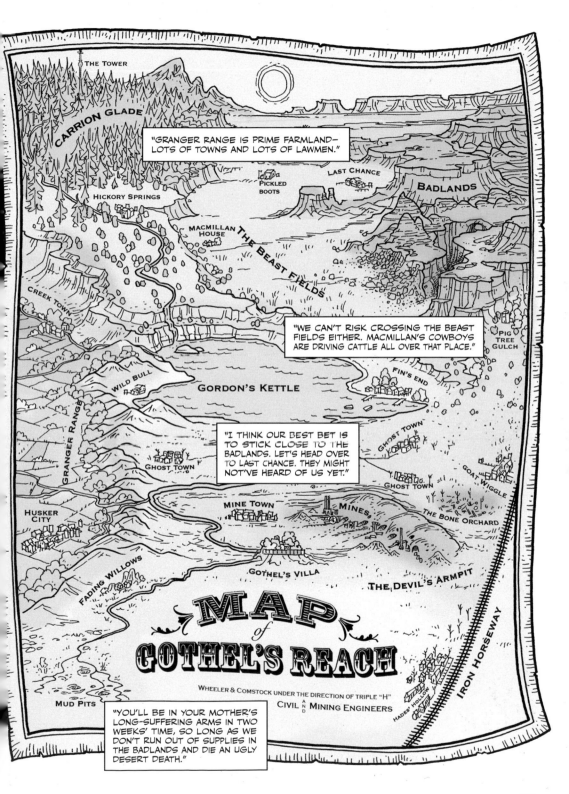

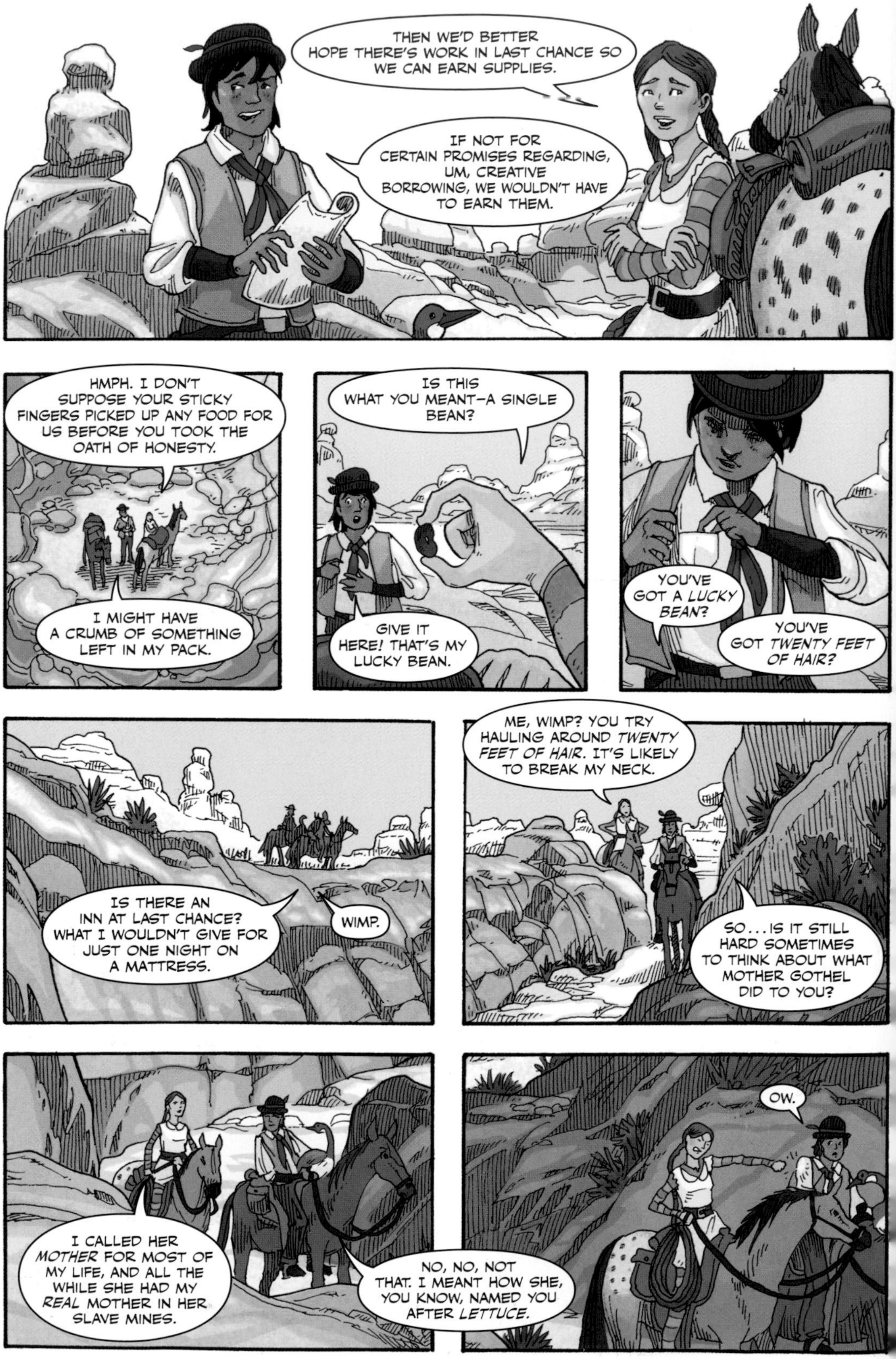
THEN WE'D BETTER HOPE THERE'S WORK IN LAST CHANCE SO WE CAN EARN SUPPLIES.
IF NOT FOR CERTAIN PROMISES REGARDING, UM, CREATIVE BORROWING, WE WOULDN'T HAVE TO EARN THEM.
HMPH. I DON'T SUPPOSE YOUR STICKY FINGERS PICKED UP ANY FOOD FOR US BEFORE YOU TOOK THE OATH OF HONESTY.
I MIGHT HAVE A CRUMB OF SOMETHING LEFT IN MY PACK.
IS THIS WHAT YOU MEANT–A SINGLE BEAN?
GIVE IT HERE! THAT'S MY LUCKY BEAN.
YOU'VE GOT A *LUCKY BEAN*?
YOU'VE GOT *TWENTY FEET OF HAIR?*
IS THERE AN INN AT LAST CHANCE? WHAT I WOULDN'T GIVE FOR JUST ONE NIGHT ON A MATTRESS.
WIMP.
ME, WIMP? YOU TRY HAULING AROUND *TWENTY FEET OF HAIR*. IT'S LIKELY TO BREAK MY NECK.
SO . . . IS IT STILL HARD SOMETIMES TO THINK ABOUT WHAT MOTHER GOTHEL DID TO YOU?
I CALLED HER *MOTHER* FOR MOST OF MY LIFE, AND ALL THE WHILE SHE HAD MY *REAL* MOTHER IN HER SLAVE MINES.
NO, NO, NOT THAT. I MEANT HOW SHE, YOU KNOW, NAMED YOU AFTER *LETTUCE*.
OW.

Last Chance was quiet. Almost too quiet.

IT'S QUIET.

ALMOST TOO QUIET.

On second thought, it was just plain quiet.

YOU THINK THEY KNOW WE'RE HORSE-STEALING OUTLAWS?

THERE'S YOUR ANSWER.

WANTED
DEAD or ALIVE
RAPUNZEL

FOR HORSE THIEVING, KIDNAPPING, JAIL BREAKING, AND USING HER HAIR IN A MANNER OTHER THAN NATURE INTENDED!

REWARD

CLICK!

CLICK!

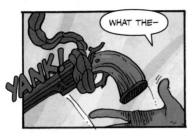

WHAT THE—

YANK!

SNAP!

CRASH!

DAG-NABIT!

I was noticing how without guns in their hands...

I RECKON YOU'D BETTER LEAVE MY FRIEND ALONE.

...most folk around here turned pale.

Made me realize I'd never seen Jack touch a gun except to throw it away.

WOW. I MEAN, WOW.

I JUST...HE MADE ME MAD, AND I THOUGHT HE WAS GOING TO SHOOT YOU.

I DIDN'T MEAN TO.

PUNZIE, I CAN'T WAIT TO SEE WHAT YOU'LL DO WHEN YOU ACTUALLY MEAN TO.

83

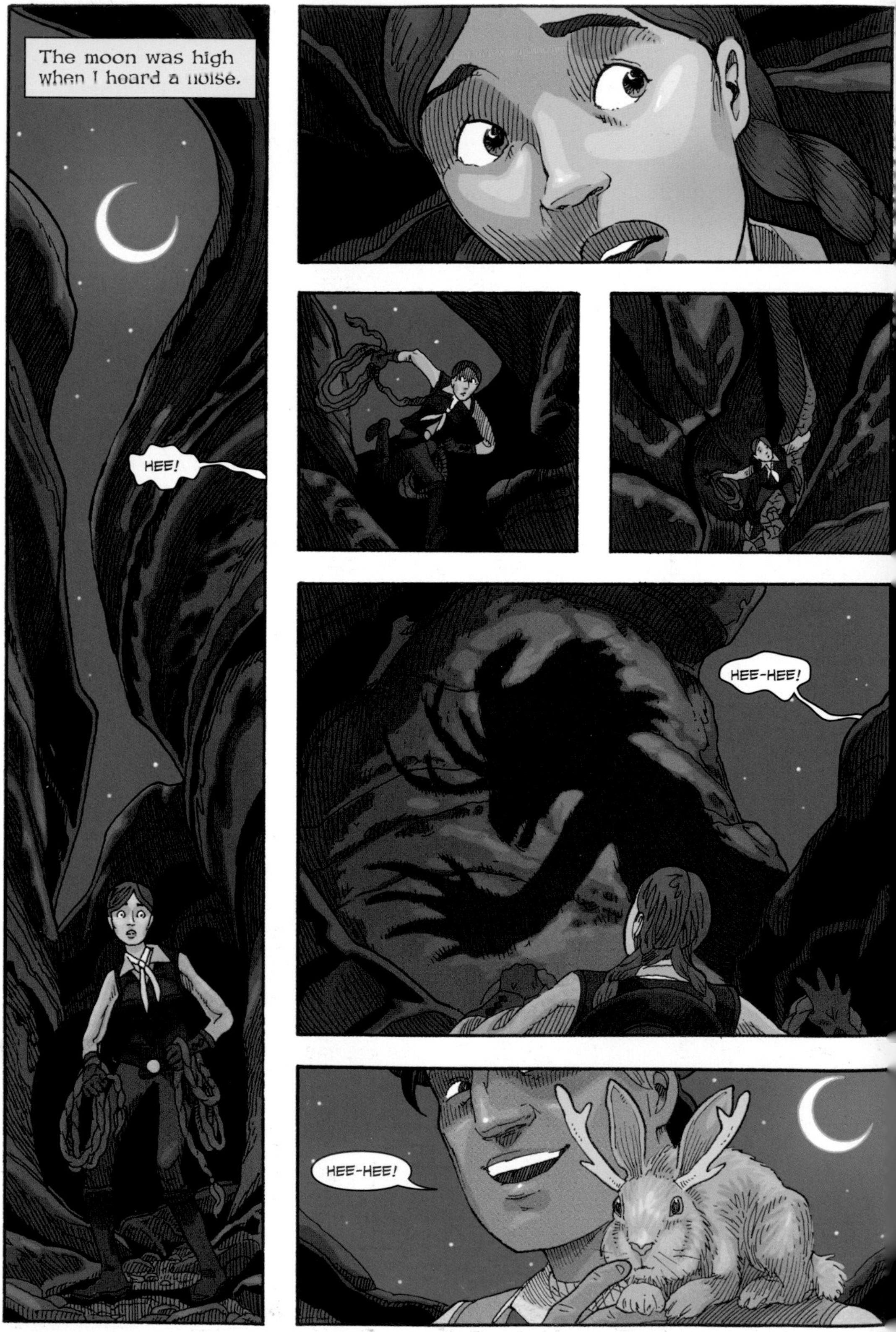
The moon was high when I heard a noise.
HEE!
HEE-HEE!
HEE-HEE!

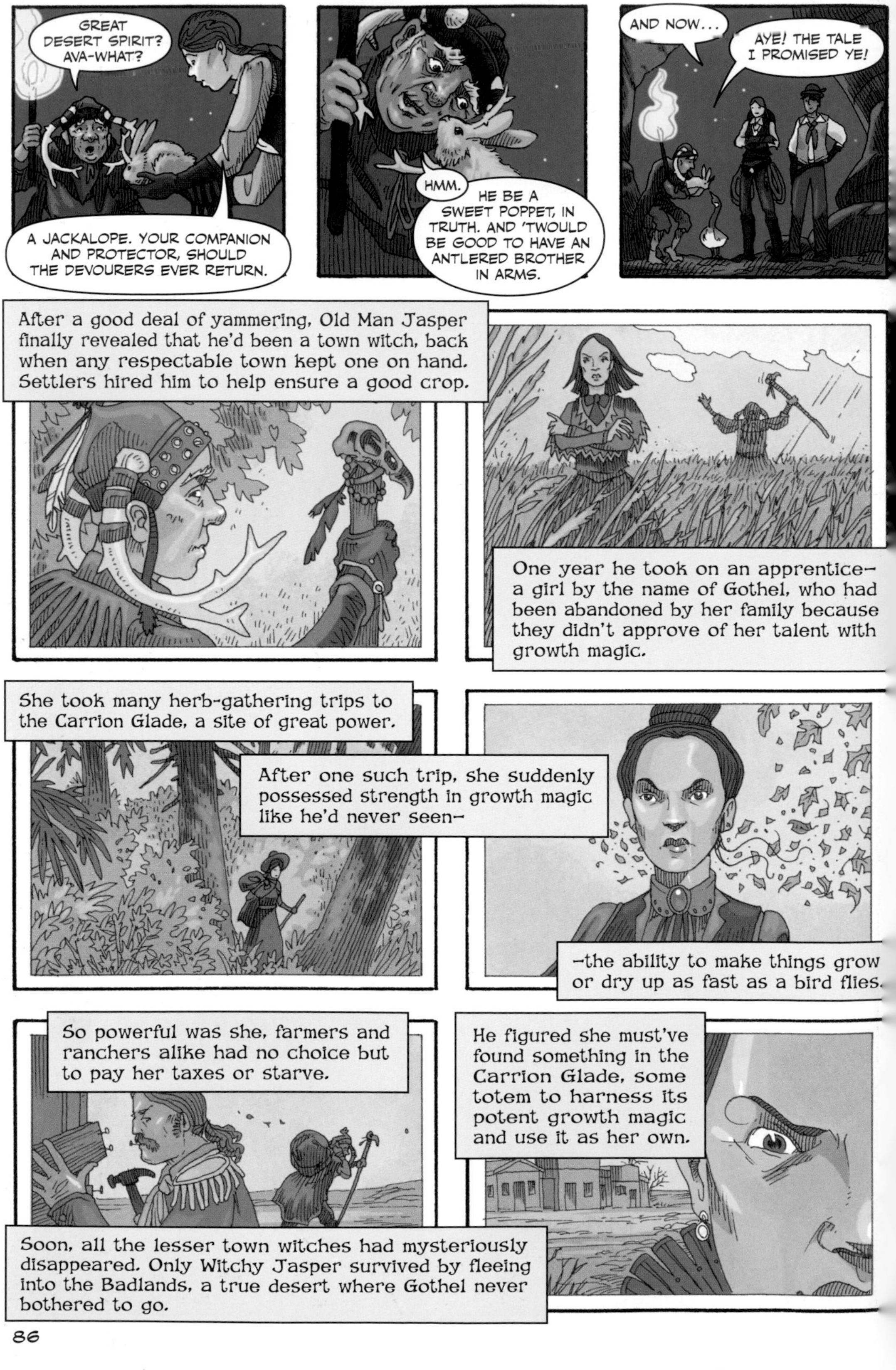
GREAT DESERT SPIRIT? AVA-WHAT?
A JACKALOPE. YOUR COMPANION AND PROTECTOR, SHOULD THE DEVOURERS EVER RETURN.
HMM.
HE BE A SWEET POPPET, IN TRUTH. AND 'TWOULD BE GOOD TO HAVE AN ANTLERED BROTHER IN ARMS.
AND NOW...
AYE! THE TALE I PROMISED YE!
After a good deal of yammering, Old Man Jasper finally revealed that he'd been a town witch, back when any respectable town kept one on hand. Settlers hired him to help ensure a good crop.
One year he took on an apprentice—a girl by the name of Gothel, who had been abandoned by her family because they didn't approve of her talent with growth magic.
She took many herb-gathering trips to the Carrion Glade, a site of great power.
After one such trip, she suddenly possessed strength in growth magic like he'd never seen—
—the ability to make things grow or dry up as fast as a bird flies.
So powerful was she, farmers and ranchers alike had no choice but to pay her taxes or starve.
He figured she must've found something in the Carrion Glade, some totem to harness its potent growth magic and use it as her own.
Soon, all the lesser town witches had mysteriously disappeared. Only Witchy Jasper survived by fleeing into the Badlands, a true desert where Gothel never bothered to go.

87

LIKE I SAID, I DON'T HAVE MANY FRIENDS, AND NONE OF THEM...

I felt like there was more to say, but I didn't know what it was.

...NONE OF THEM ARE QUITE LIKE YOU.

Three days later, our food bags picked clean of the crumbs, and our poor horse worn out, we rode into Pig Tree Gulch.

GOOD MORNING, GENTLE FOLK!

WE ARE A COUPLE OF WANDERING HEROES, HERE TO OFFER OUR HUMBLE SERVICES TO YOUR FINE TOWN.

THE NAME'S LACEY. I GUESS YOU CAN TALK TO ME. WOULD YOU FOLKS BE ON MOTHER GOTHEL'S PAYROLL?

NO, MA'AM, I'M AFRAID WE'RE WANTED, DEAD OR ALIVE.

WELL, THAT'S OKAY, THEN. WE'VE BEEN LUCKY OUT HERE SO FAR—GOTHEL'S TAX COLLECTORS HAVEN'T COME IN YEARS, AND WE COULDN'T PAY 'EM IF THEY DID.

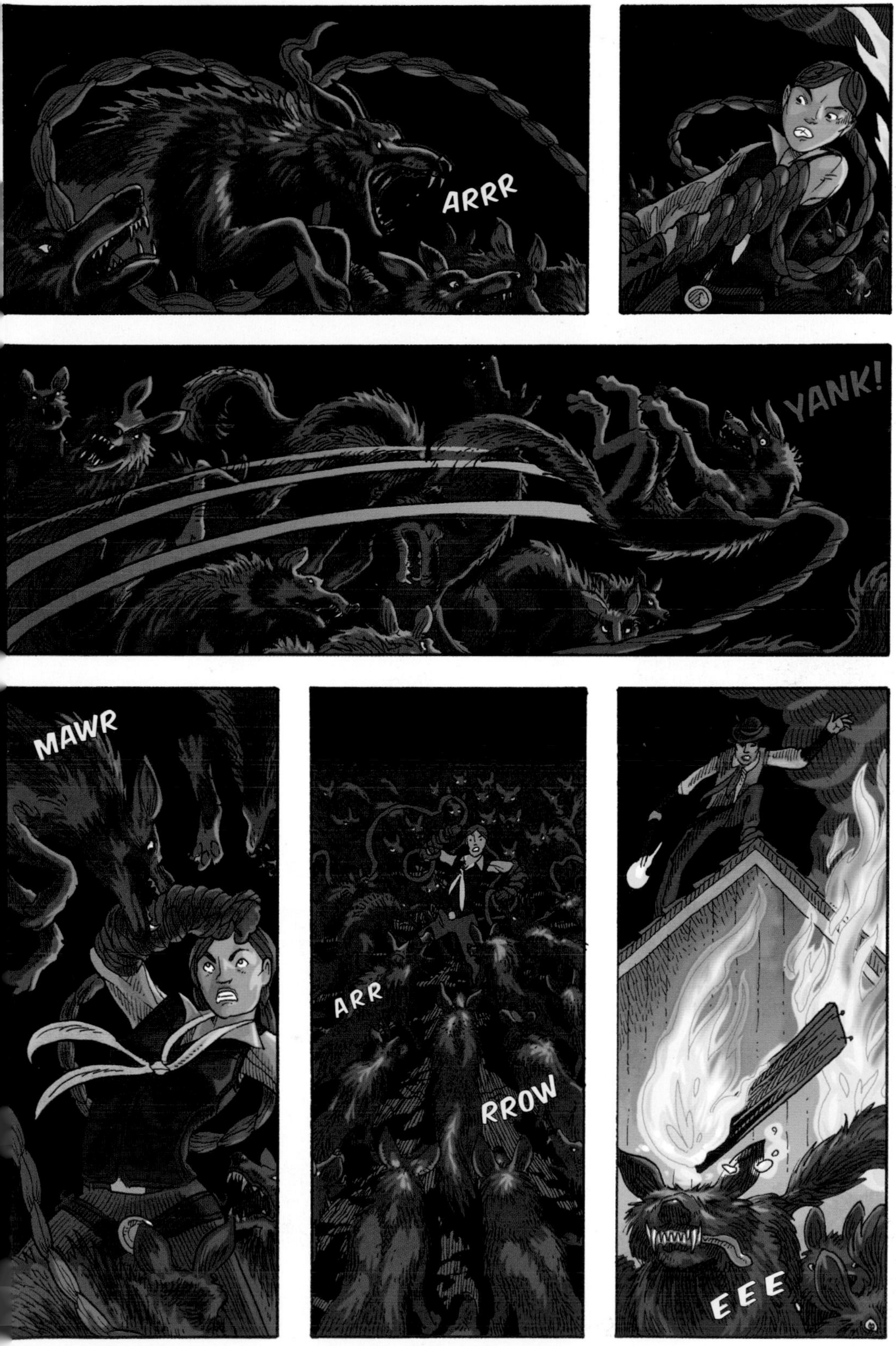
ARRR
YANK!
MAWR
ARR
RROW
EEE

94

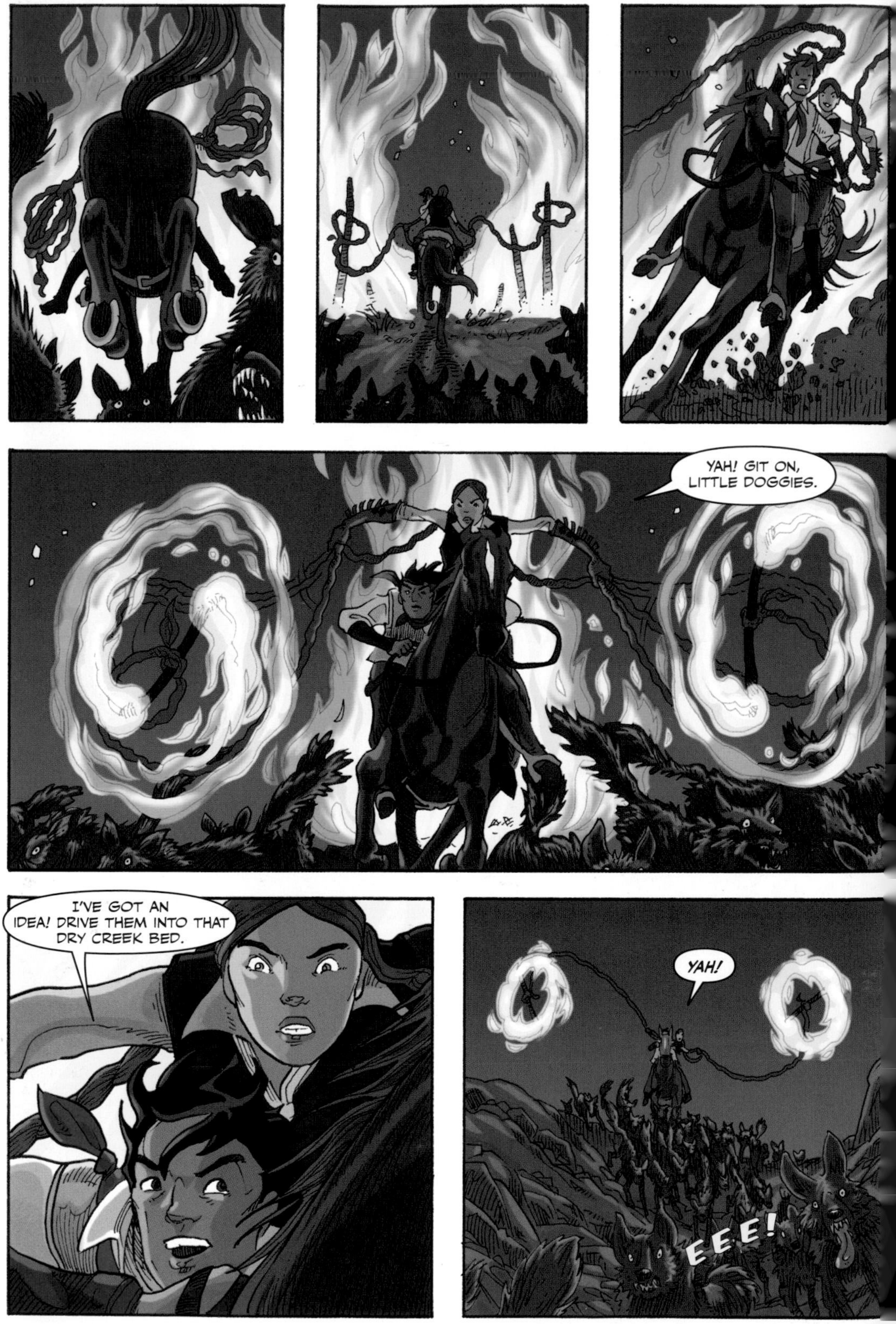
YAH! GIT ON, LITTLE DOGGIES.
I'VE GOT AN IDEA! DRIVE THEM INTO THAT DRY CREEK BED.
YAH!
EEE!

We drove those critters for a good hour, Jack claiming any minute we'd reach the border of Gothel's Reach.

WHEN I CAME TO GOTHEL'S REACH ON THE IRON HORSEWAY, WE PASSED LOTS OF PRAIRIE.

I FIGURE HER POWER REACHES ONLY SO FAR. IF WE GET BEYOND IT, WE MIGHT FIND SOME LAND...

...HER POWER NEVER TOUCHED.

WHOA. SO THIS IS WHAT PIG TREE GULCH WOULD LOOK LIKE IF GOTHEL HADN'T DRIED UP THAT LAND.

IT WASN'T NATURAL THE WAY THOSE COYOTES WERE ACTING. THEY'LL BE BETTER OFF AWAY FROM ANYTHING TOUCHED BY GOTHEL'S MAGIC.

WOULDN'T WE ALL.

LEAN AGAINST ME AND SLEEP IF YOU CAN, AND I'LL GUIDE THE HORSE BACK.

REALLY? YOU DON'T MIND?

I DON'T MIND A WHIT.

LANDS, BUT I'M PLUMB TIRED.

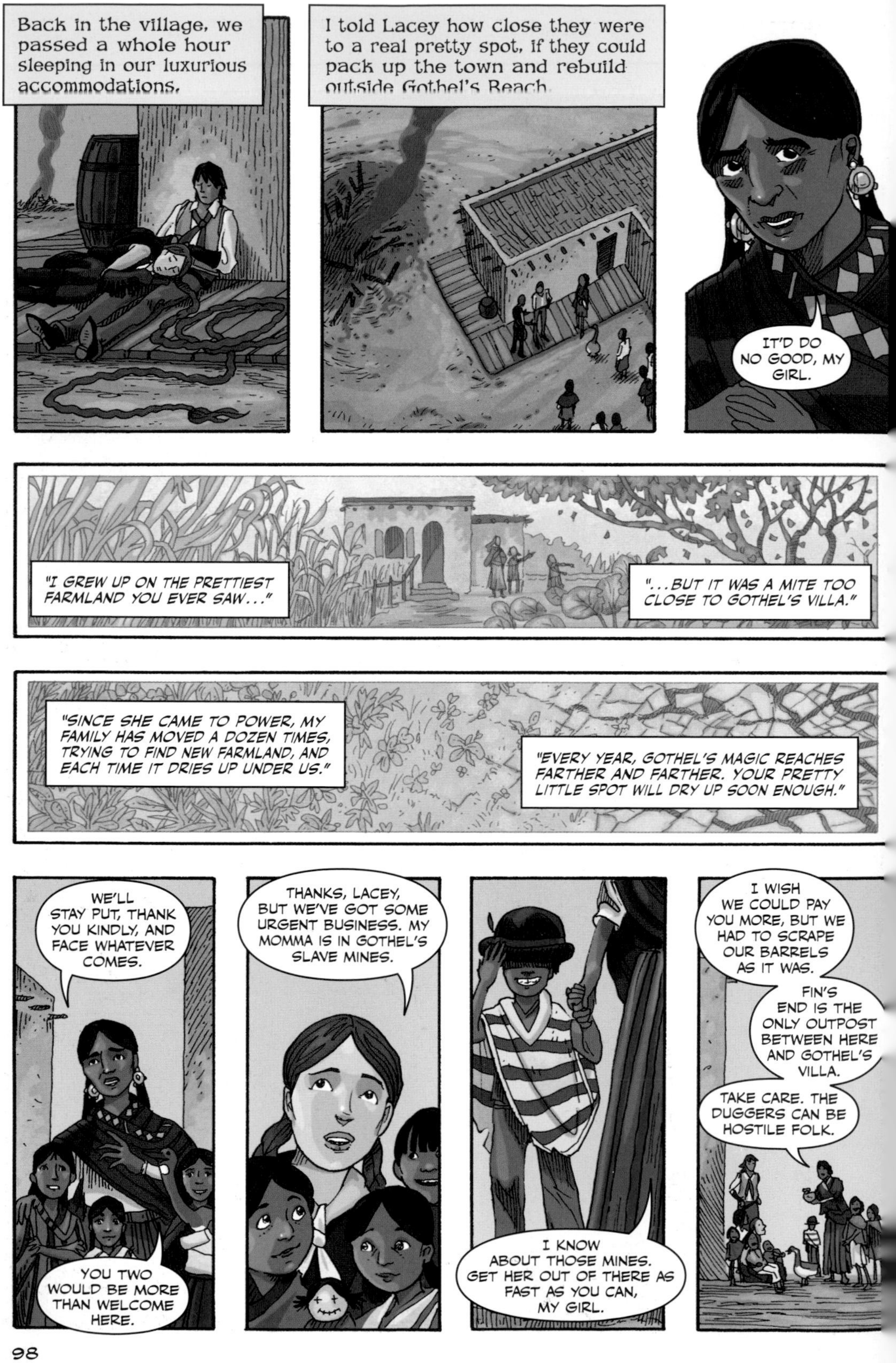

Back in the village, we passed a whole hour sleeping in our luxurious accommodations.
I told Lacey how close they were to a real pretty spot, if they could pack up the town and rebuild outside Gothel's Reach.
IT'D DO NO GOOD, MY GIRL.
"I GREW UP ON THE PRETTIEST FARMLAND YOU EVER SAW..."
"...BUT IT WAS A MITE TOO CLOSE TO GOTHEL'S VILLA."
"SINCE SHE CAME TO POWER, MY FAMILY HAS MOVED A DOZEN TIMES, TRYING TO FIND NEW FARMLAND, AND EACH TIME IT DRIES UP UNDER US."
"EVERY YEAR, GOTHEL'S MAGIC REACHES FARTHER AND FARTHER. YOUR PRETTY LITTLE SPOT WILL DRY UP SOON ENOUGH."
WE'LL STAY PUT, THANK YOU KINDLY, AND FACE WHATEVER COMES.
YOU TWO WOULD BE MORE THAN WELCOME HERE.
THANKS, LACEY, BUT WE'VE GOT SOME URGENT BUSINESS. MY MOMMA IS IN GOTHEL'S SLAVE MINES.
I KNOW ABOUT THOSE MINES. GET HER OUT OF THERE AS FAST AS YOU CAN, MY GIRL.
I WISH WE COULD PAY YOU MORE, BUT WE HAD TO SCRAPE OUR BARRELS AS IT WAS.
FIN'S END IS THE ONLY OUTPOST BETWEEN HERE AND GOTHEL'S VILLA.
TAKE CARE. THE DUGGERS CAN BE HOSTILE FOLK.

101

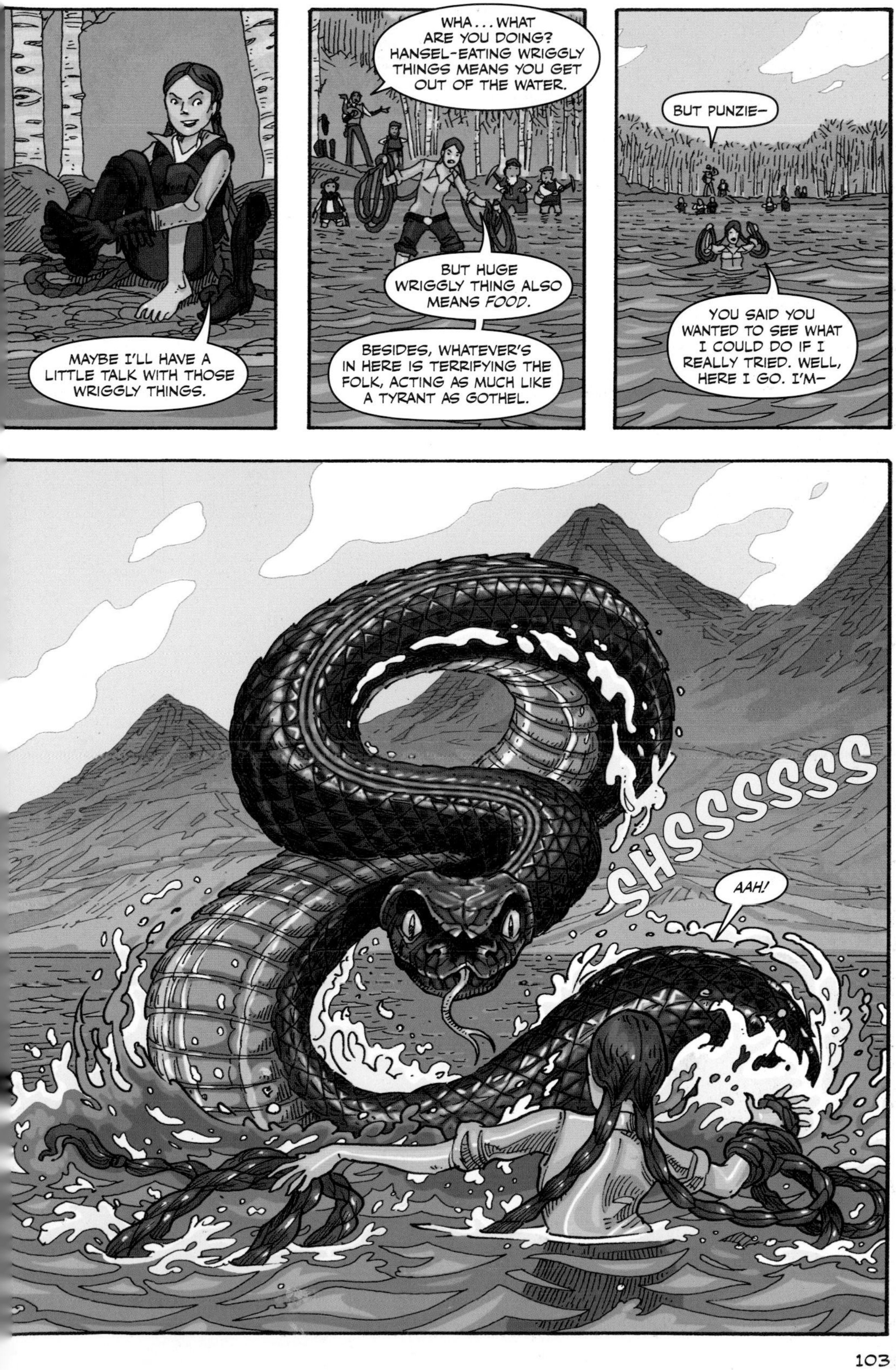
MAYBE I'LL HAVE A LITTLE TALK WITH THOSE WRIGGLY THINGS.
WHA...WHAT ARE YOU DOING? HANSEL-EATING WRIGGLY THINGS MEANS YOU GET OUT OF THE WATER.
BUT HUGE WRIGGLY THING ALSO MEANS *FOOD*.
BESIDES, WHATEVER'S IN HERE IS TERRIFYING THE FOLK, ACTING AS MUCH LIKE A TYRANT AS GOTHEL.
BUT PUNZIE—
YOU SAID YOU WANTED TO SEE WHAT I COULD DO IF I REALLY TRIED. WELL, HERE I GO. I'M—
SHSSSSSS
AAH!

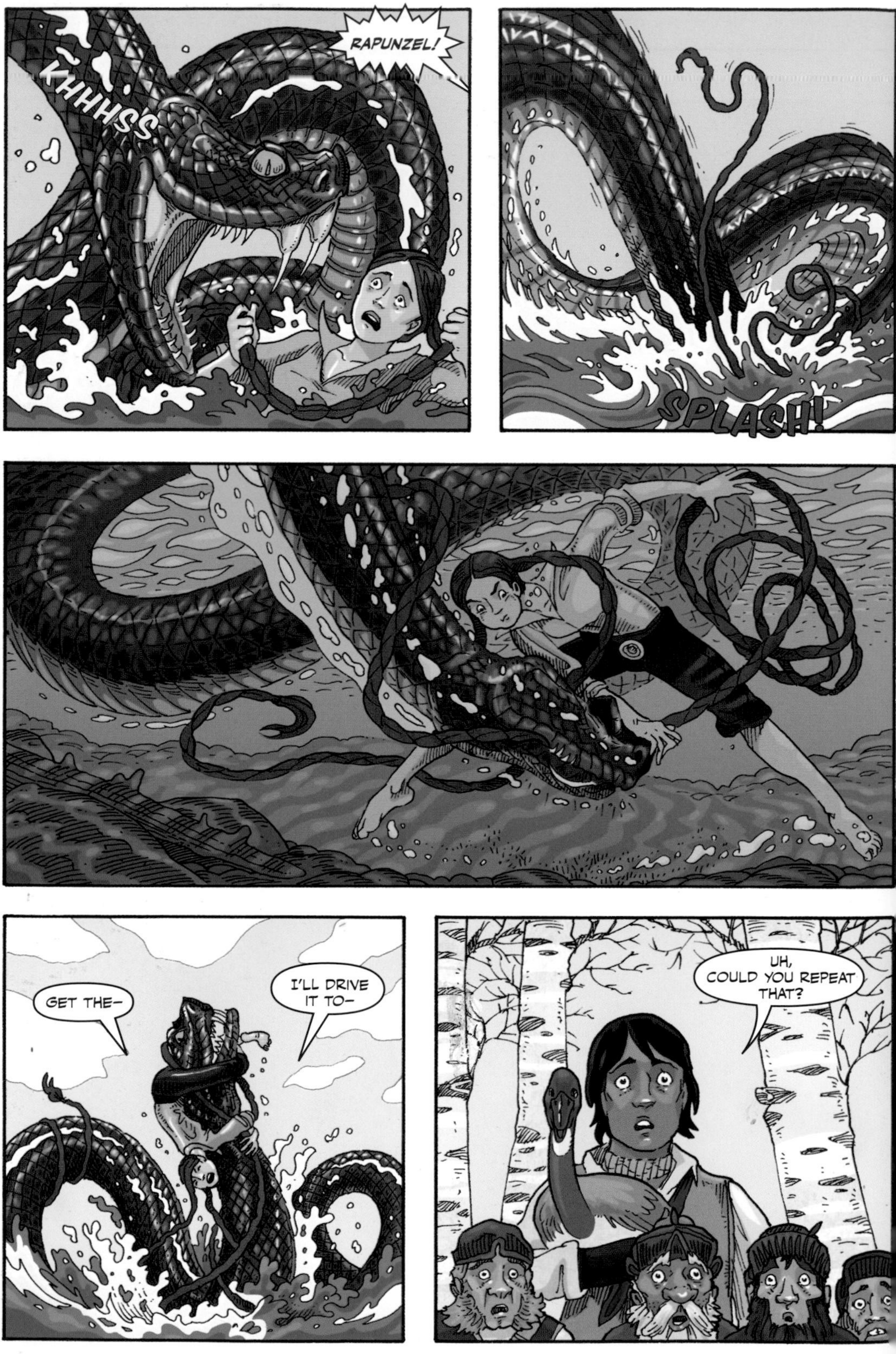
KHHHSS
RAPUNZEL!
SPLASH!
GET THE–
I'LL DRIVE IT TO–
UH, COULD YOU REPEAT THAT?

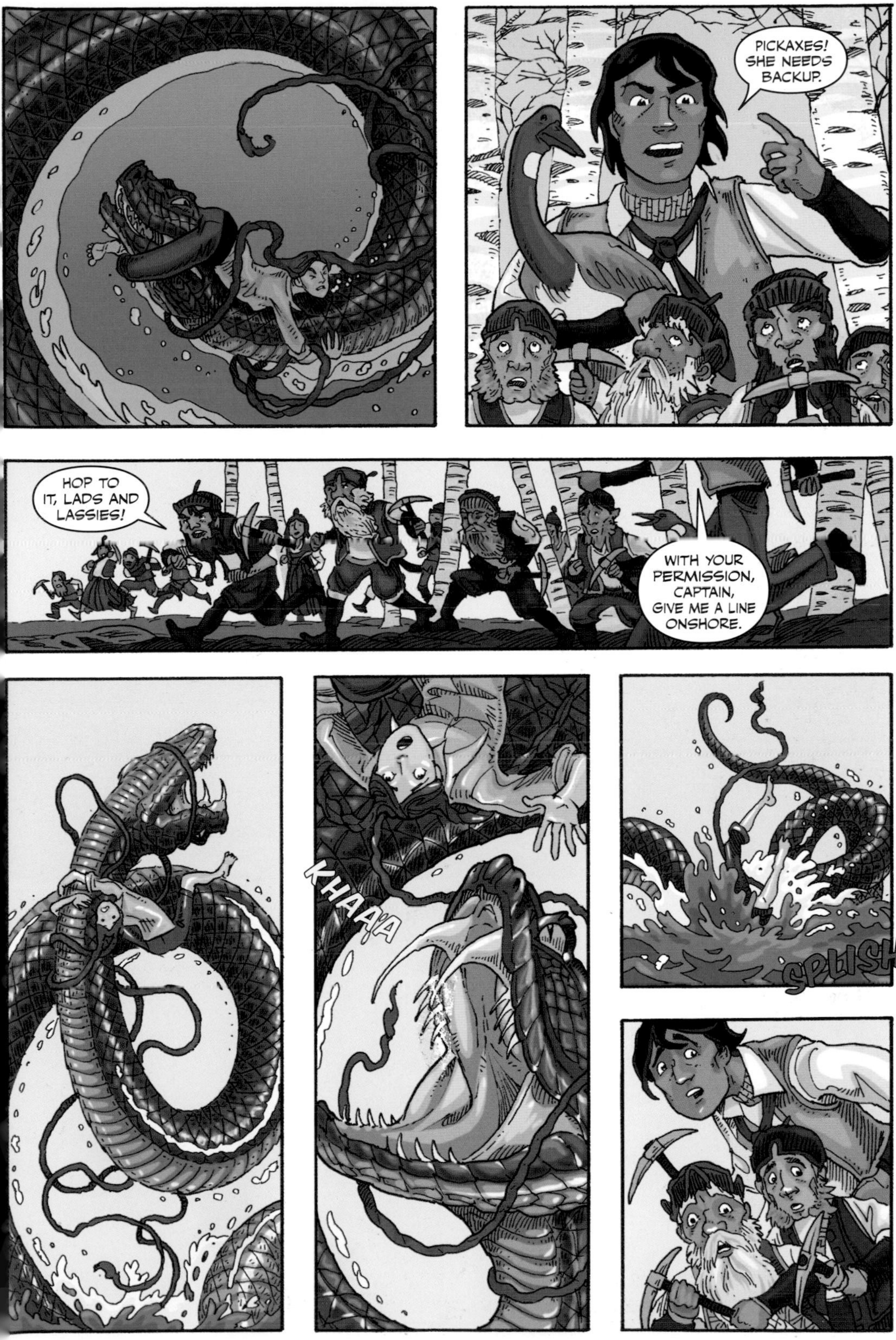
PICKAXES! SHE NEEDS BACKUP.
HOP TO IT, LADS AND LASSIES!
WITH YOUR PERMISSION, CAPTAIN, GIVE ME A LINE ONSHORE.
KHAAA
SPLISH

ost of the serpent went to the smoking sheds, enough to last them weeks, and the head made quite a feast.

HURRAH FOR OUR NEW FRIENDS!

HURRAH!

IN SHOW OF OUR GRATITUDE, WE WISH TO PRESENT YOU WITH INGA!

OO OOOH.

HEY, JACK, THEY'RE GIVING YOU A WIFE.

BEHOLD *INGA!* PICK OF ALL PICKS!

BREAKER OF THE UNBREAKABLE!

WHOA. THANKS.

THE FASTEST WAY WOULD BE GORDON'S KETTLE DOWN TO THE RIVER, BUT...

THE BOAT WENT AWAY WITH BRUTE.

YOU COULD TAKE *MY* BOAT!

UM, I'M THINKING I MIGHT BE AFRAID OF THE WATER...

HEY, ME TOO!

IN THAT CASE, YOU FOLKS WILL HAVE TO RIDE THROUGH...THE DEVIL'S ARMPIT!

Now, with a name like the Devil's Armpit, you'd think it'd be a right jolly place.

We didn't sleep much at night.

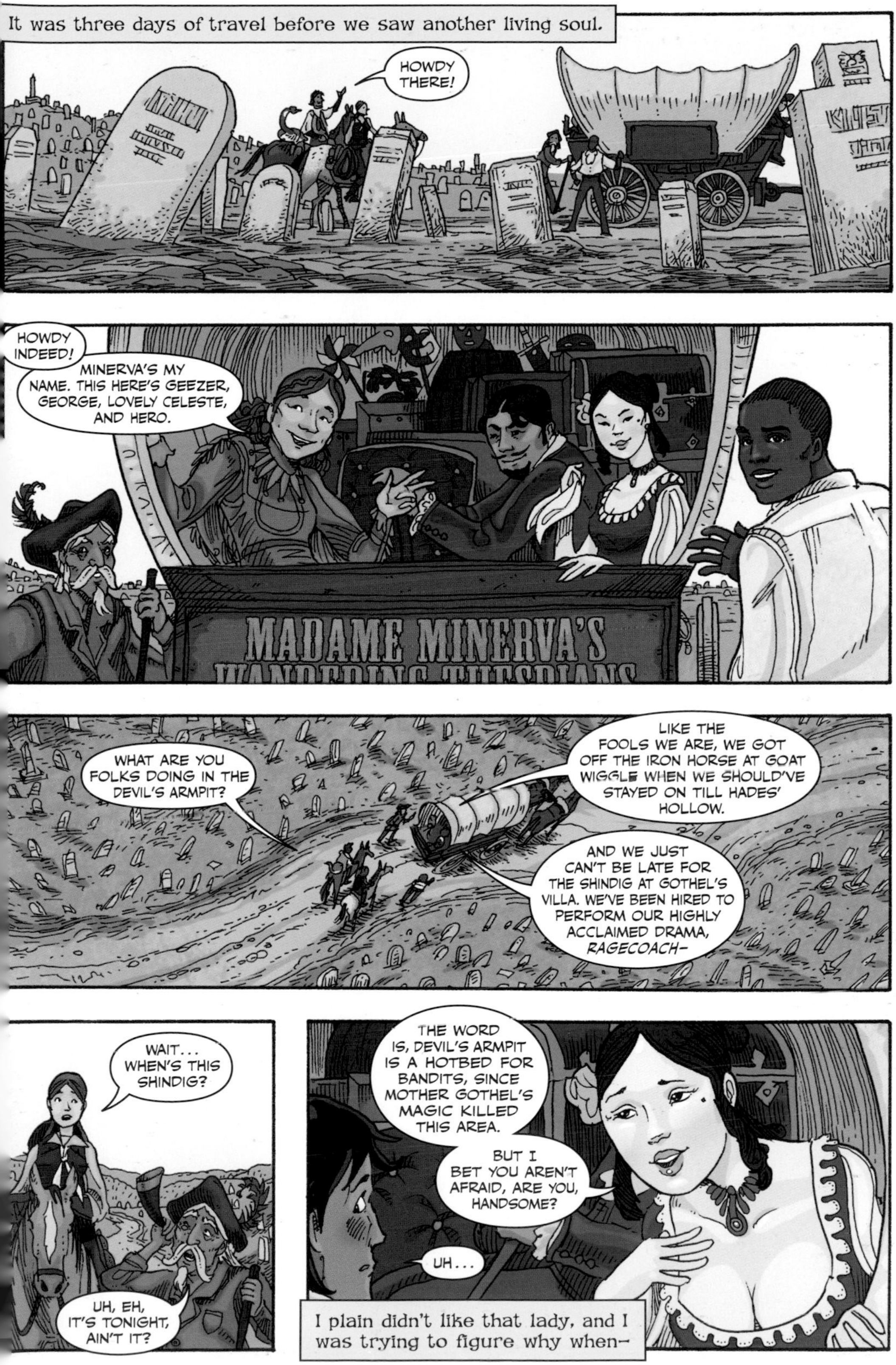

It was three days of travel before we saw another living soul.
HOWDY THERE!
HOWDY INDEED!
MINERVA'S MY NAME. THIS HERE'S GEEZER, GEORGE, LOVELY CELESTE, AND HERO.
MADAME MINERVA'S
WHAT ARE YOU FOLKS DOING IN THE DEVIL'S ARMPIT?
LIKE THE FOOLS WE ARE, WE GOT OFF THE IRON HORSE AT GOAT WIGGLE WHEN WE SHOULD'VE STAYED ON TILL HADES' HOLLOW.
AND WE JUST CAN'T BE LATE FOR THE SHINDIG AT GOTHEL'S VILLA. WE'VE BEEN HIRED TO PERFORM OUR HIGHLY ACCLAIMED DRAMA, *RAGECOACH*–
WAIT... WHEN'S THIS SHINDIG?
UH, EH, IT'S TONIGHT, AIN'T IT?
THE WORD IS, DEVIL'S ARMPIT IS A HOTBED FOR BANDITS, SINCE MOTHER GOTHEL'S MAGIC KILLED THIS AREA.
BUT I BET YOU AREN'T AFRAID, ARE YOU, HANDSOME?
UH...
I plain didn't like that lady, and I was trying to figure why when–

SOMEONE CALL FOR TROUBLE?

THAT HAPPENS TO BE THE SPECIALTY OF TINA'S TERRIBLE TRIO.

ARRRH!

HOLD IT THERE, ER...*TINA.* WE'RE PROTECTING THIS CONVOY OF ENTERTAINMENT.

WELL, *SHE* IS ANYWAY.

BEEFEATER, YOU AND YOKUM KEEP YOUR GUNS POINTED AT ANYTHING THAT MOVES, AND I'LL JUST HAVE A LOOK-SEE IN THAT WAGON.

IGNORE 'EM, BOYS. THEY'RE NOT EVEN ARMED.

There was a time when I might have been scared of those clowns.

But since tussling with a rampaging boar...

WHACK!

CRACK!

...a pack of outlaw kidnappers...

...a horde of blood-hungry coyotes and a sea serpent...

...well, Tina's Terrible Trio just didn't raise my hackles

WE'RE OUT-WOMANED, FELLAS! BACK TO THE LAIR!

ZIP

110

HUZZAH, HUZZAH!

OH, YOU WERE SO BRAVE!

NAH, I WAS JUST...IT WAS ALL PUNZIE.

WELL, I'M ALL TO PIECES GRATEFUL TO YOU, MY POPPET, AND YOU JUST NAME A FAVOR. ANYTHING!

ACTUALLY, THERE IS SOMETHING... WE NEED TO GET INTO GOTHEL'S VILLA, BUT A SHINDIG MEANS SHE'LL HAVE LOTS MORE GUARDS.

DO YOU THINK YOU COULD SNEAK US IN?

FOR YOU, MY DARLING GIRL, WE WON'T JUST GET YOU INTO THE SHINDIG...

WE'LL MAKE YOU THE BELLE OF THE BALL!

We got the troupe on their way to the Villa with a plan to meet up that night. I had a matter to take care of first.

WHAT IF SHE DOESN'T WANT ME? WHAT IF SHE'S DEAD? WHAT IF—

HEY, WHAT MOTHER IN THE WORLD WOULDN'T WANT A BRAID-WHIPPING DAUGHTER?

SHE'S OKAY. IT'S GOING TO BE GREAT.

VILLA

MINES

111

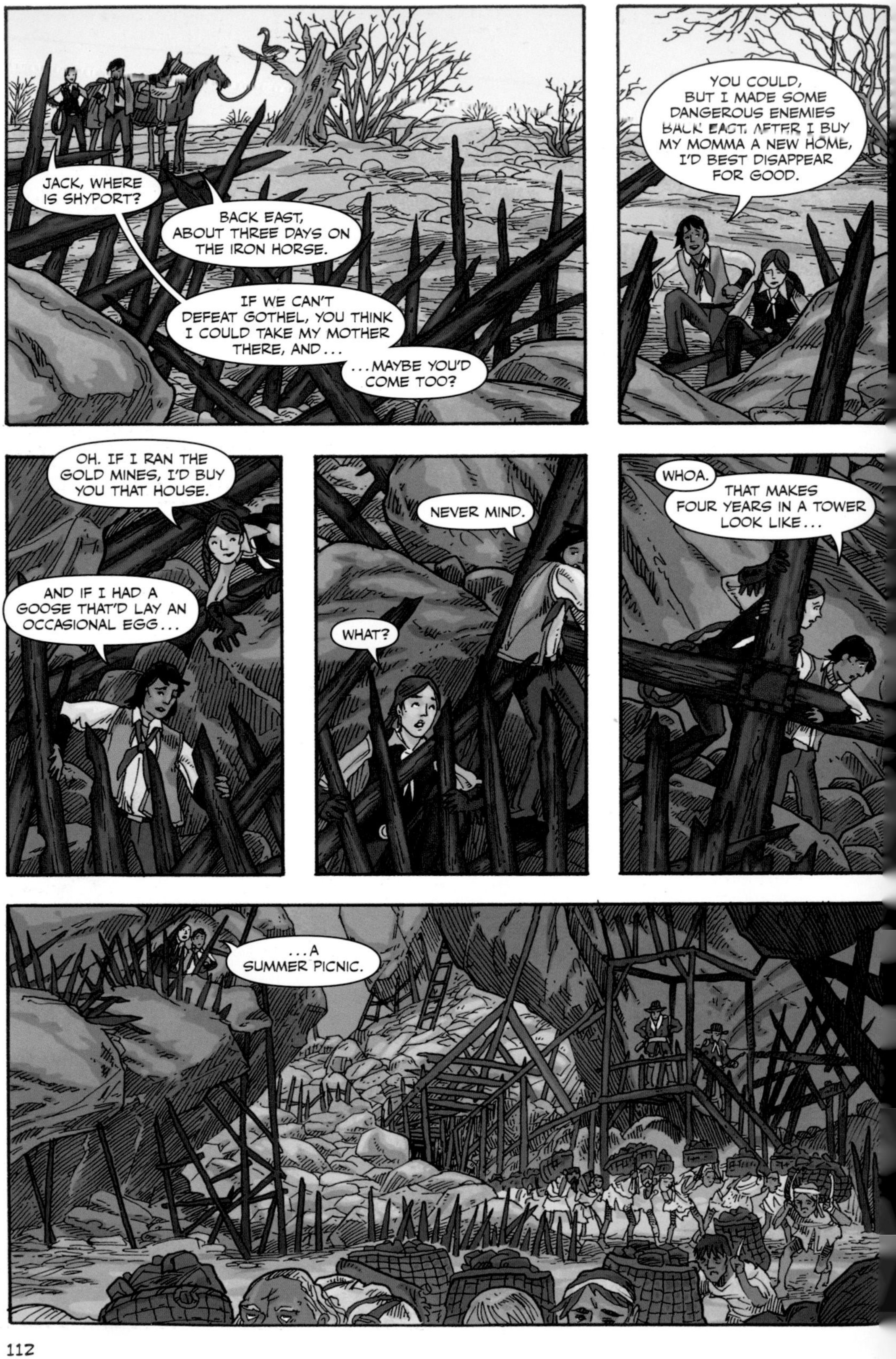
JACK, WHERE IS SHYPORT?
BACK EAST, ABOUT THREE DAYS ON THE IRON HORSE.
IF WE CAN'T DEFEAT GOTHEL, YOU THINK I COULD TAKE MY MOTHER THERE, AND...
...MAYBE YOU'D COME TOO?
YOU COULD, BUT I MADE SOME DANGEROUS ENEMIES BACK EAST. AFTER I BUY MY MOMMA A NEW HOME, I'D BEST DISAPPEAR FOR GOOD.
OH. IF I RAN THE GOLD MINES, I'D BUY YOU THAT HOUSE.
AND IF I HAD A GOOSE THAT'D LAY AN OCCASIONAL EGG...
NEVER MIND.
WHAT?
WHOA.
THAT MAKES FOUR YEARS IN A TOWER LOOK LIKE...
...A SUMMER PICNIC.

HEY, I KNOW HIM!

ERK!

HI MASON! SORRY, I HOPE I DIDN'T HURT YOU.

RAPUNZEL, IS THAT YOU? YOU'RE OKAY!

YOU'VE PICKED A HECK OF A TIME TO COME BACK. TONIGHT'S THE YEARLY SHINDIG, WHEN ALL THE CATTLE AND FARMING FOLK PAY HER TAXES AND PRETEND THEY'RE THRILLED SHE'S IN CHARGE.

TYPICAL RICH-FOLK FANFARE.

THIS IS JACK. HE HELPED ME GET HERE TO LOOK FOR MY MOTHER. DO YOU KNOW WHICH CAMP—

SOON AS GOTHEL GOT A MAGI-GRAPH ABOUT YOUR ESCAPE, SHE LOCKED YOUR MOTHER IN THE VILLA'S DUNGEON.

WHY THAT EVIL-EYED, SCUM-GUZZLING RAT SNEAK...

RAPUNZEL, I'VE GOT TO GET BACK BEFORE I'M MISSED. IF I WERE YOU, I'D HIGHTAIL IT OUT OF HERE BEFORE THINGS TURN SOUR.

YOU'LL KEEP MUM ABOUT SEEING US?

LOOK, IF WE CAN GET IN THAT SHINDIG, I THINK I CAN MUSTER UP A QUALITY DISTRACTION THAT'LL ALLOW YOU TO SNEAK INTO THE DUNGEON.

YOU'LL JUST HAVE TO WAIT AND SEE.

OF COURSE...OH, AND GOOD WORK WITH THAT LASSO. COULDN'T HAVE DONE BETTER MYSELF.

WHAT KIND OF DISTRACTION? NOT YOU IN A DRESS, I HOPE.

And even though my life was on the line, and my mother's too, I realized I trusted him.

113

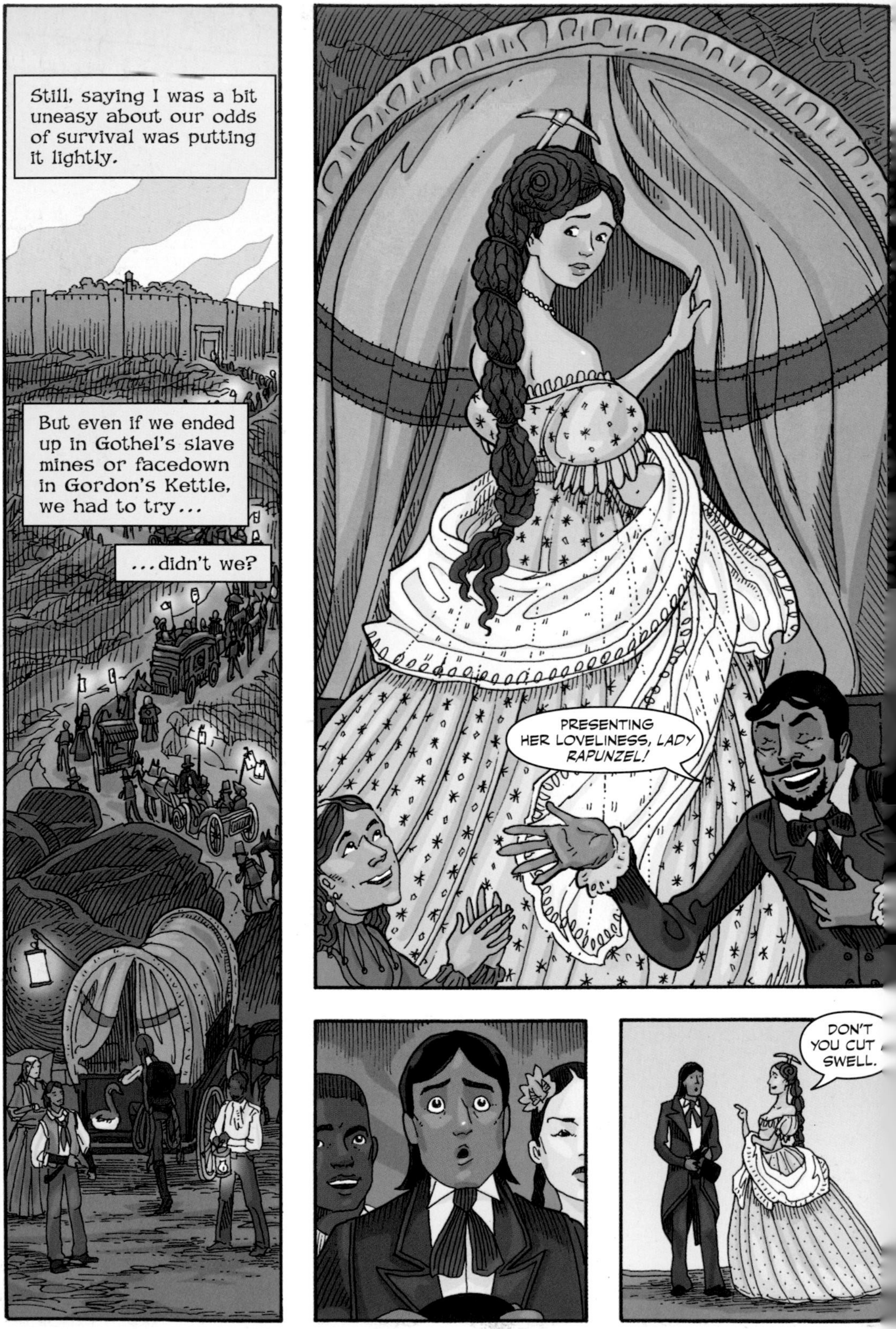
Still, saying I was a bit uneasy about our odds of survival was putting it lightly.
But even if we ended up in Gothel's slave mines or facedown in Gordon's Kettle, we had to try...
...didn't we?
PRESENTING HER LOVELINESS, *LADY RAPUNZEL!*
DON'T YOU CUT SWELL.

116

GOOD EVENING, FRIENDS.

ANOTHER PROFITABLE YEAR IN CATTLE, MINES, AND FARMS. WHEN MOTHER GOTHEL DOES WELL, YOU DO WELL.

NOW MIGHT BE A GOOD TIME FOR THAT DISTRACTION...

I'M ON IT. HEY, BE CAREFUL, OKAY?

YOU BE CAREFUL.

HURRY, JACK, PLEASE...

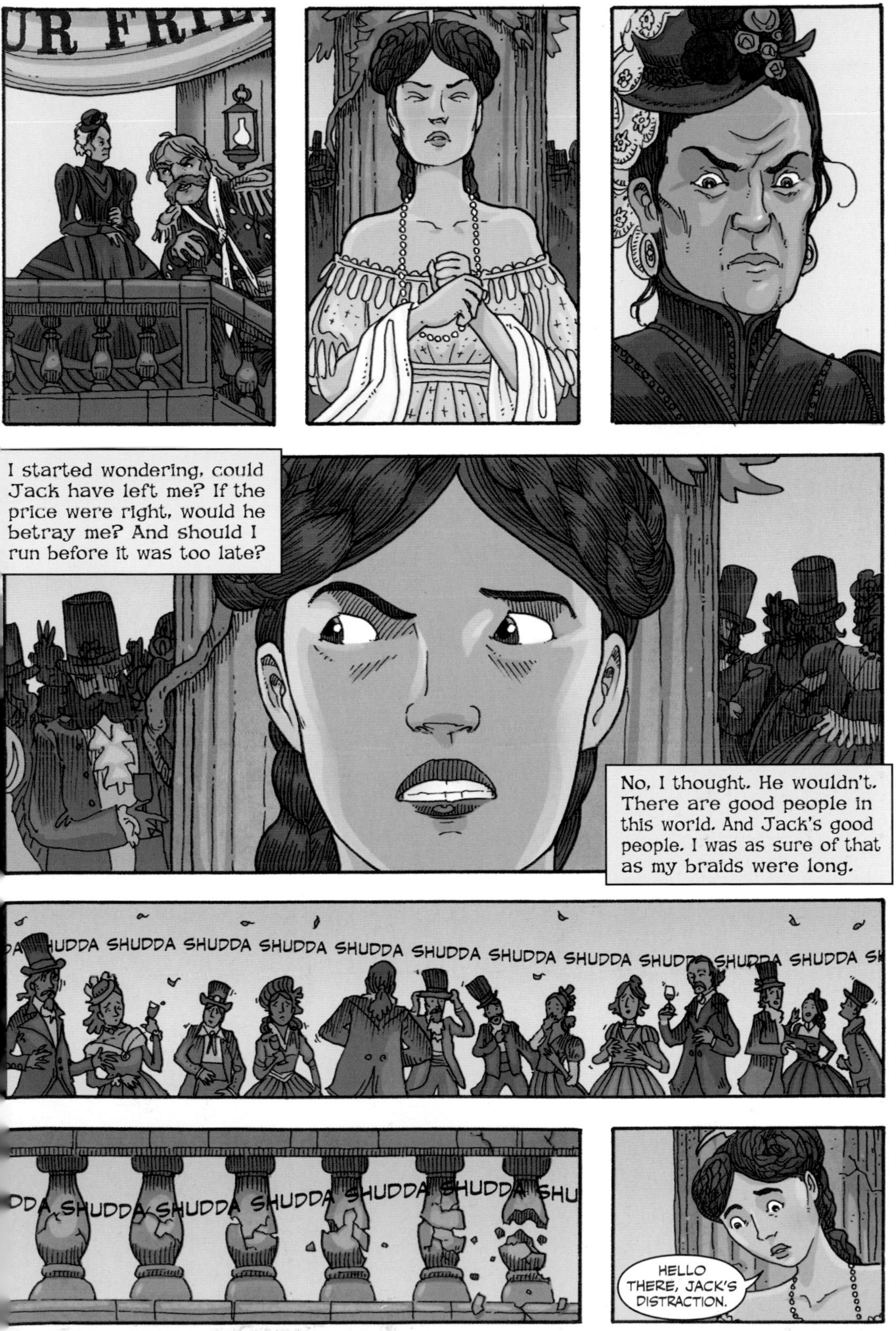
UR FRIE
I started wondering, could Jack have left me? If the price were right, would he betray me? And should I run before it was too late?
No, I thought. He wouldn't. There are good people in this world. And Jack's good people. I was as sure of that as my braids were long.
UDDA SHUDDA SHUDDA SHUDDA SHUDDA SHUDDA SHUDDA SHUDDA SHUDDA SHUDDA SHUDDA
DDA SHUDDA SHUDDA SHUDDA SHUDDA SHUDDA
HELLO THERE, JACK'S DISTRACTION.

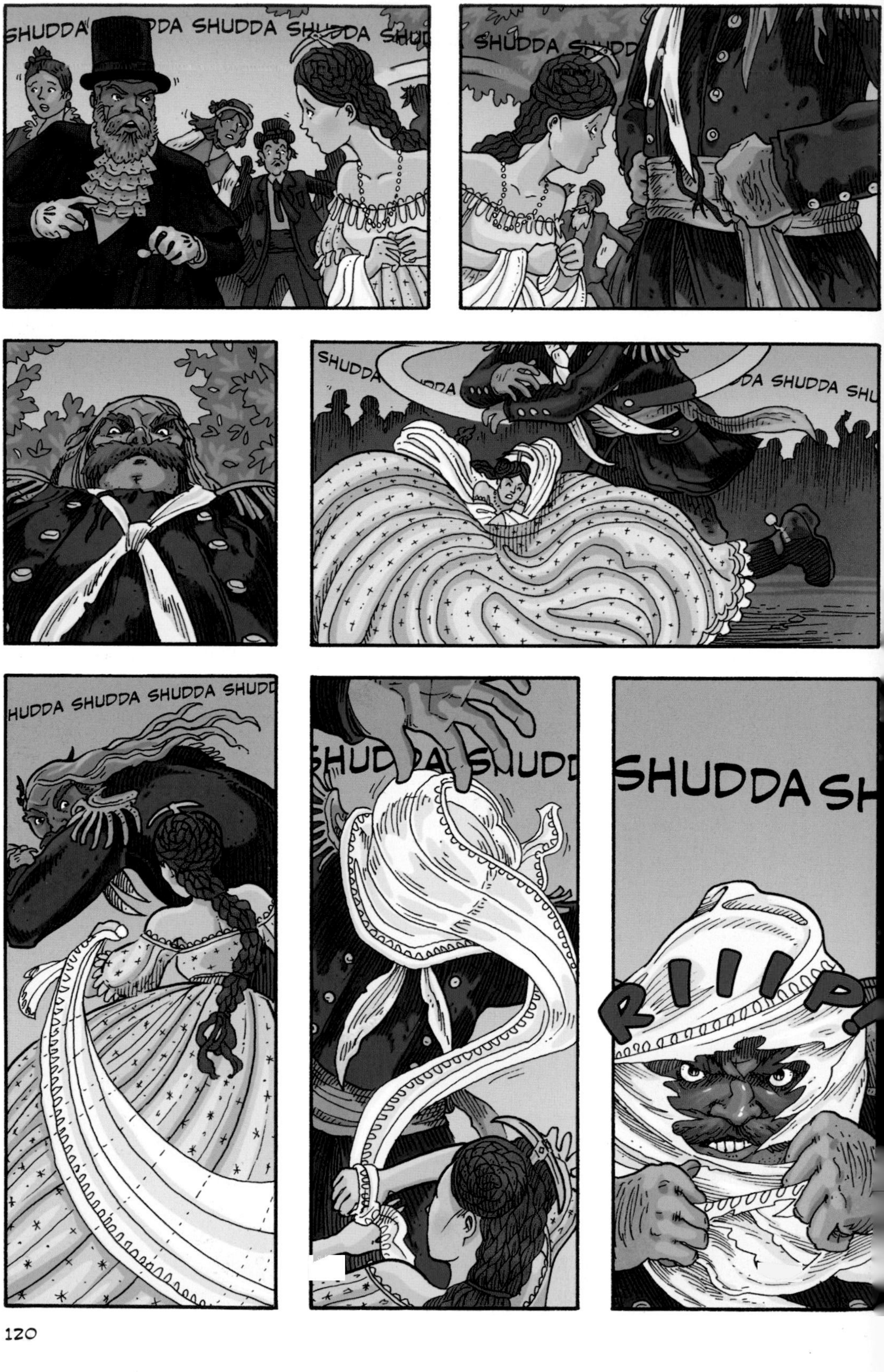
SHUDDA SHUDDA SHUDDA SHU
SHUDDA SHUDD
SHUDDA
DA SHUDDA SHU
HUDDA SHUDDA SHUDDA SHUDD
SHUDDA SHUDD
SHUDDA SH
RIIIP!

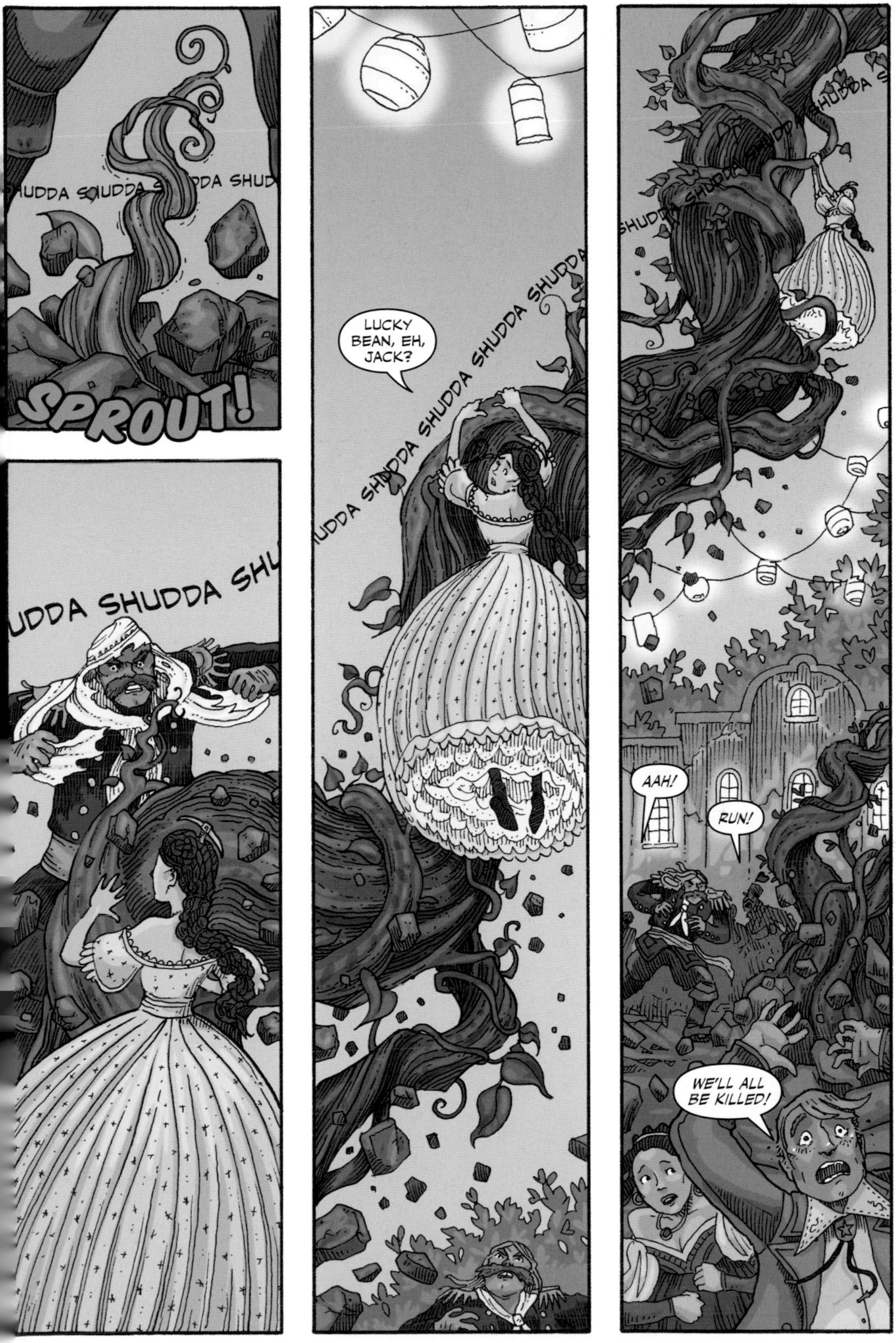
SHUDDA SHUDDA SHUDDA SHUD
SPROUT!
SHUDDA SHUDDA SHU
LUCKY BEAN, EH, JACK?
SHUDDA SHUDDA SHUDDA SHUDDA
SHUDDA SHUDDA SHUDDA SHUDDA
AAH!
RUN!
WE'LL ALL BE KILLED!

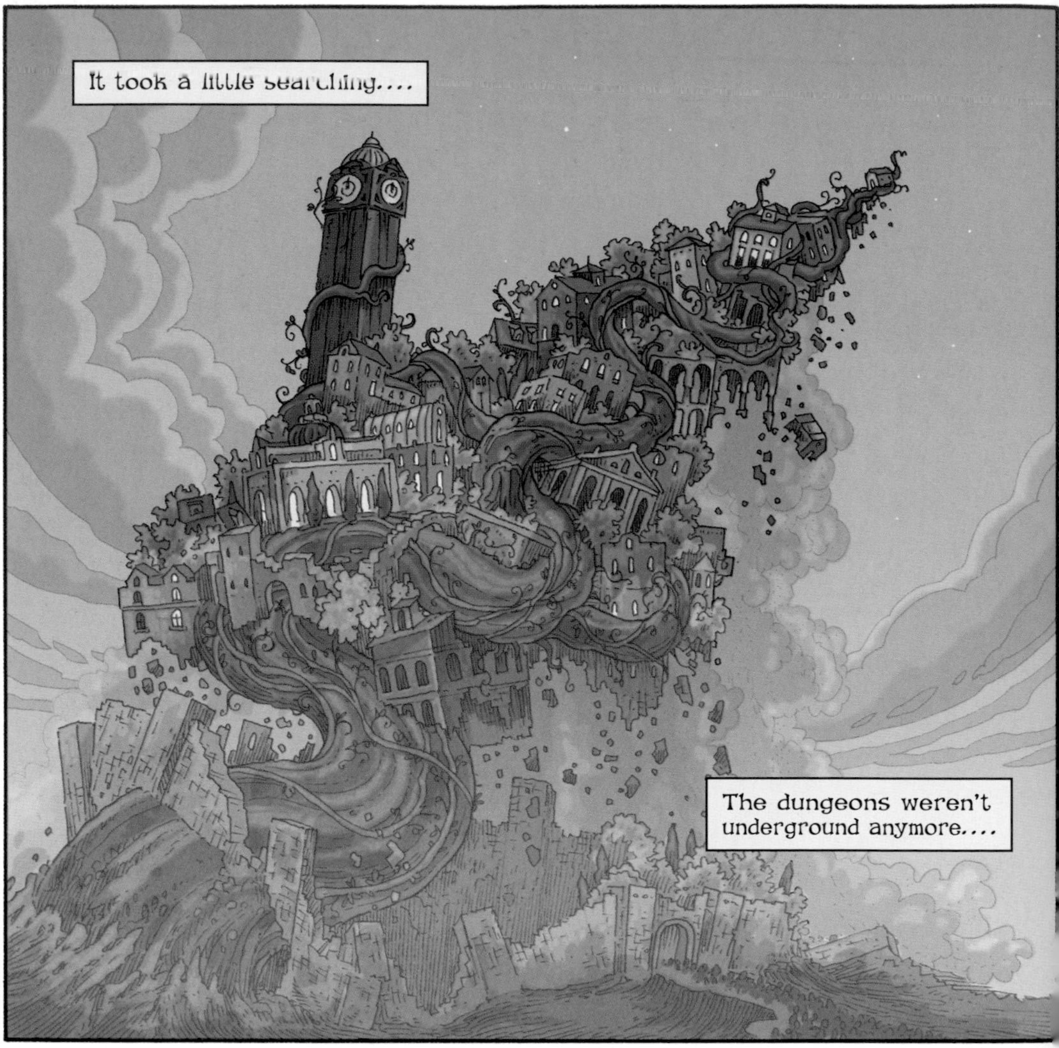
It took a little searching....
The dungeons weren't underground anymore....

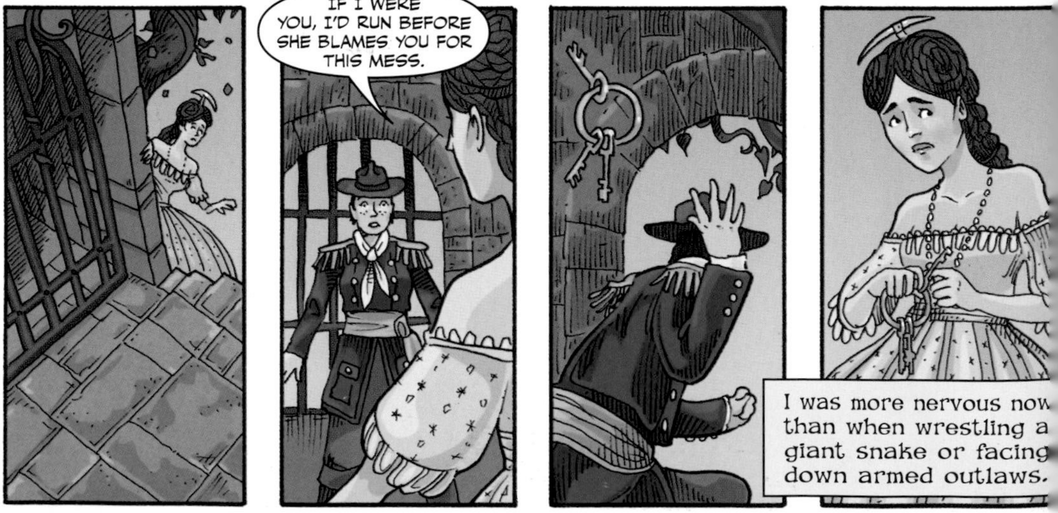
IF I WERE YOU, I'D RUN BEFORE SHE BLAMES YOU FOR THIS MESS.
I was more nervous now than when wrestling a giant snake or facing down armed outlaws.

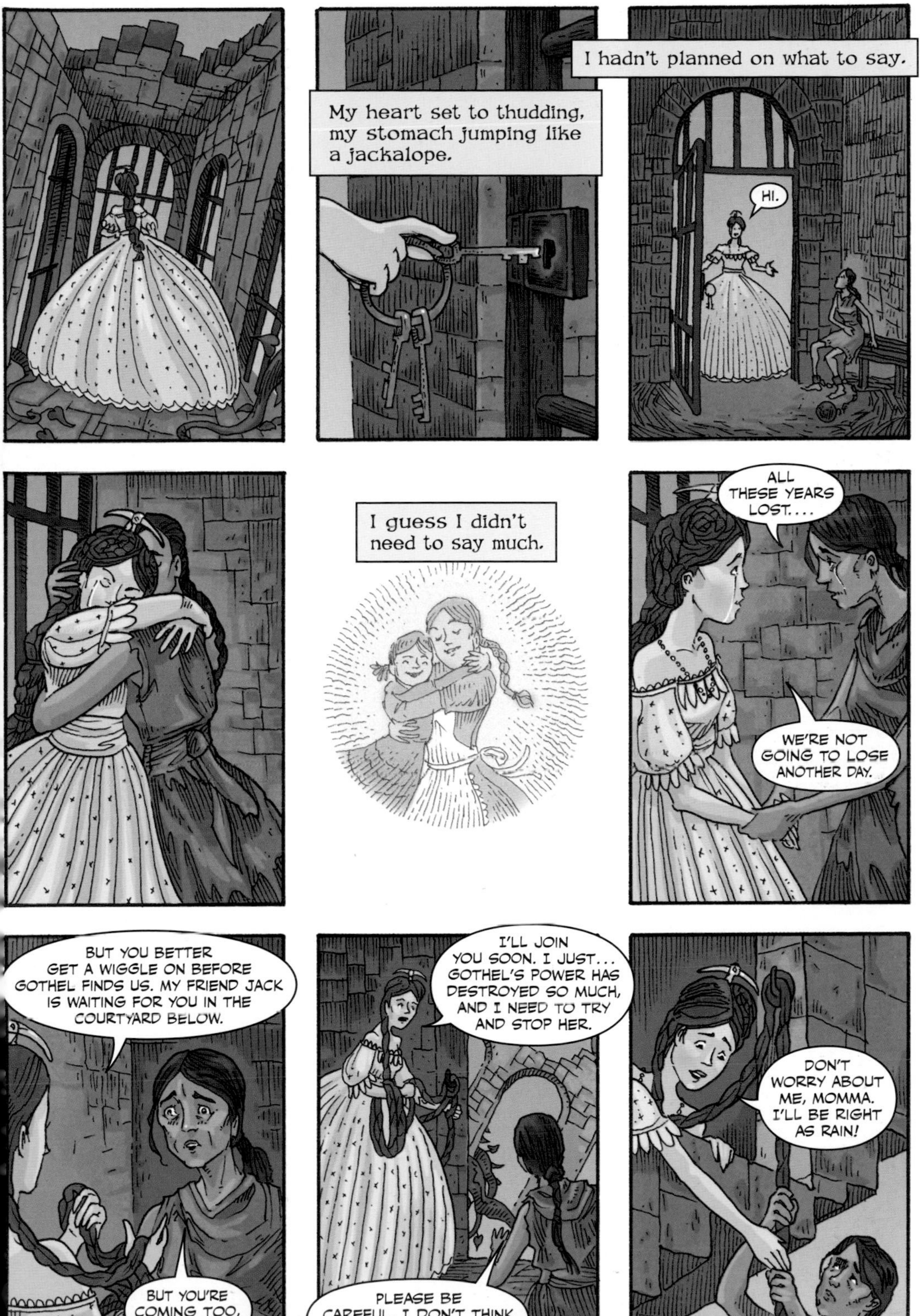

My heart set to thudding, my stomach jumping like a jackalope.
I hadn't planned on what to say.
HI.
I guess I didn't need to say much.
ALL THESE YEARS LOST. . . .
WE'RE NOT GOING TO LOSE ANOTHER DAY.
BUT YOU BETTER GET A WIGGLE ON BEFORE GOTHEL FINDS US. MY FRIEND JACK IS WAITING FOR YOU IN THE COURTYARD BELOW.
BUT YOU'RE COMING TOO, RIGHT?
I'LL JOIN YOU SOON. I JUST. . . GOTHEL'S POWER HAS DESTROYED SO MUCH, AND I NEED TO TRY AND STOP HER.
PLEASE BE CAREFUL. I DON'T THINK I COULD STAND TO LOSE YOU AGAIN.
DON'T WORRY ABOUT ME, MOMMA. I'LL BE RIGHT AS RAIN!

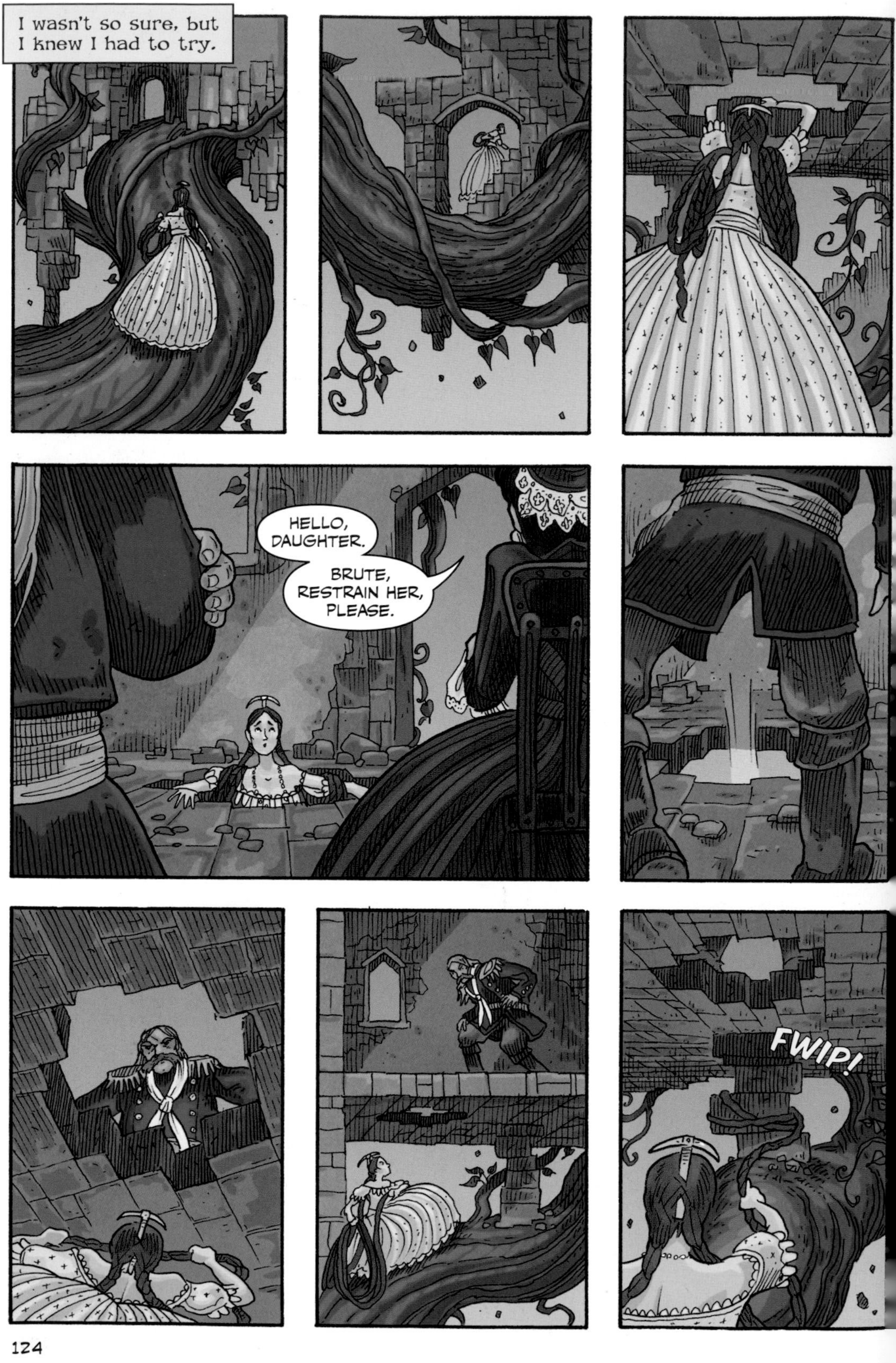
I wasn't so sure, but I knew I had to try.
HELLO, DAUGHTER.
BRUTE, RESTRAIN HER, PLEASE.
FWIP!

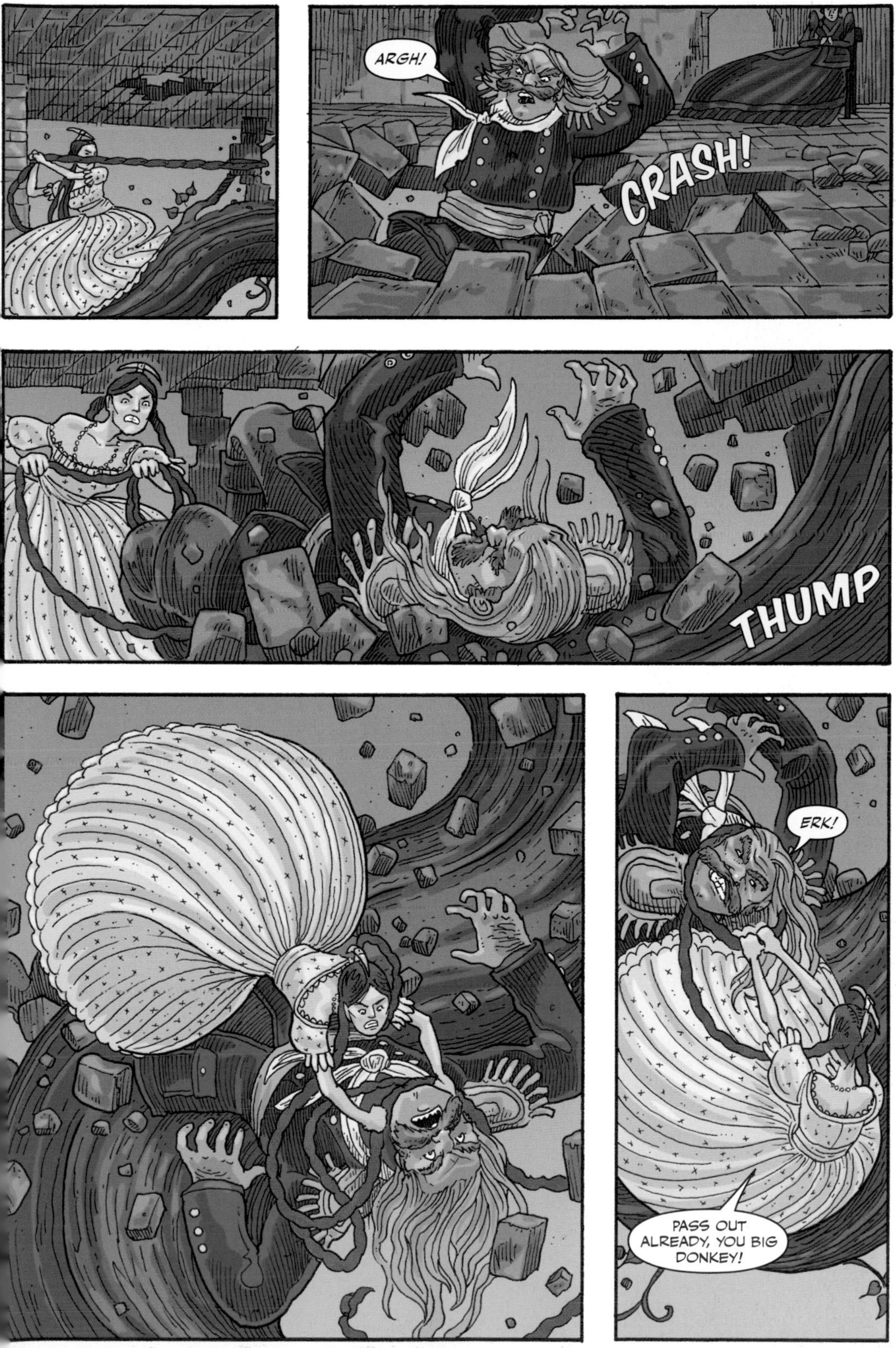
ARGH!
CRASH!
THUMP
ERK!
PASS OUT ALREADY, YOU BIG DONKEY!

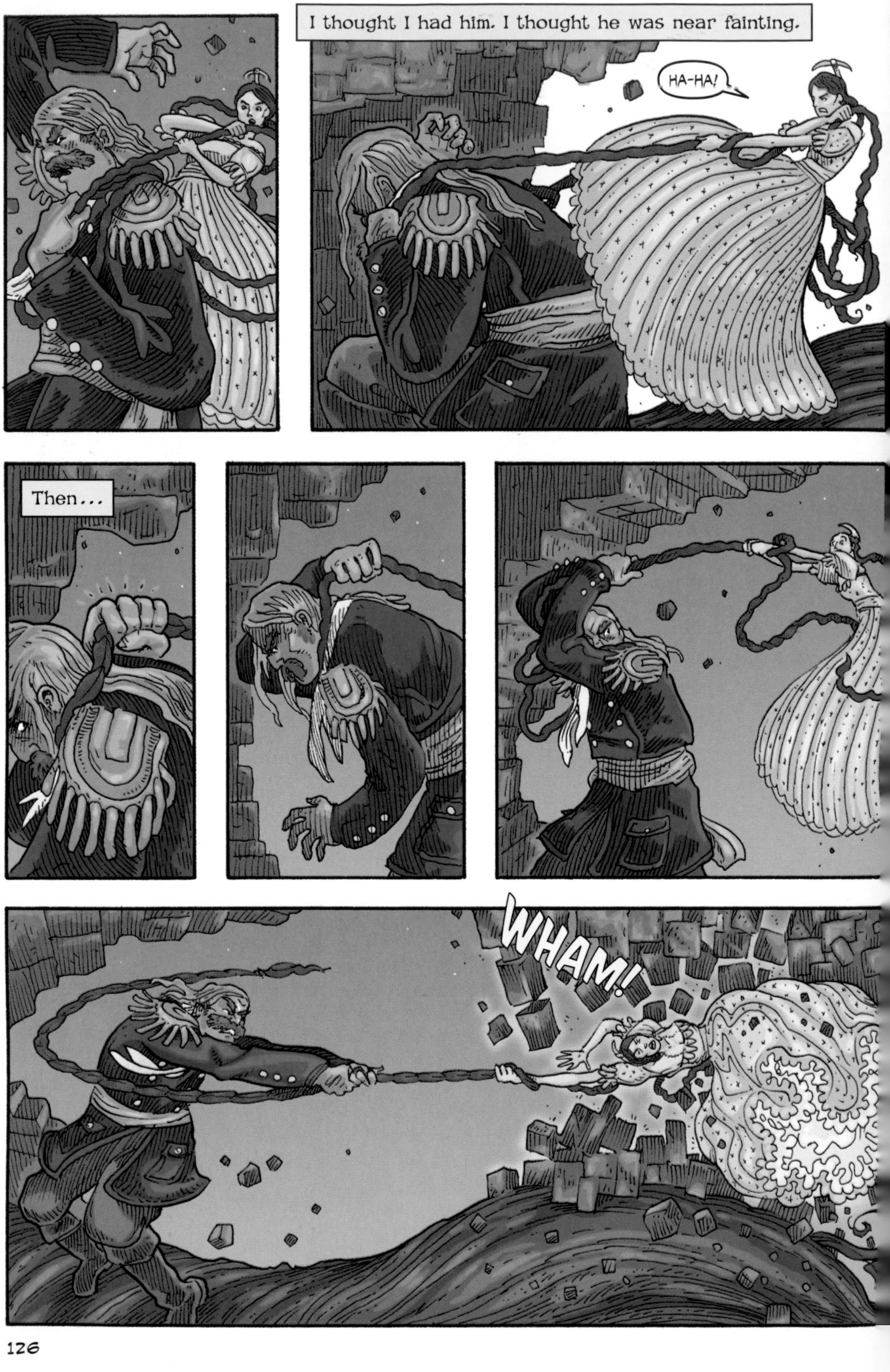
I thought I had him. I thought he was near fainting.
HA-HA!
Then...
WHAM!

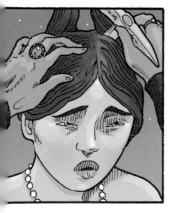

SNIP!

NO!

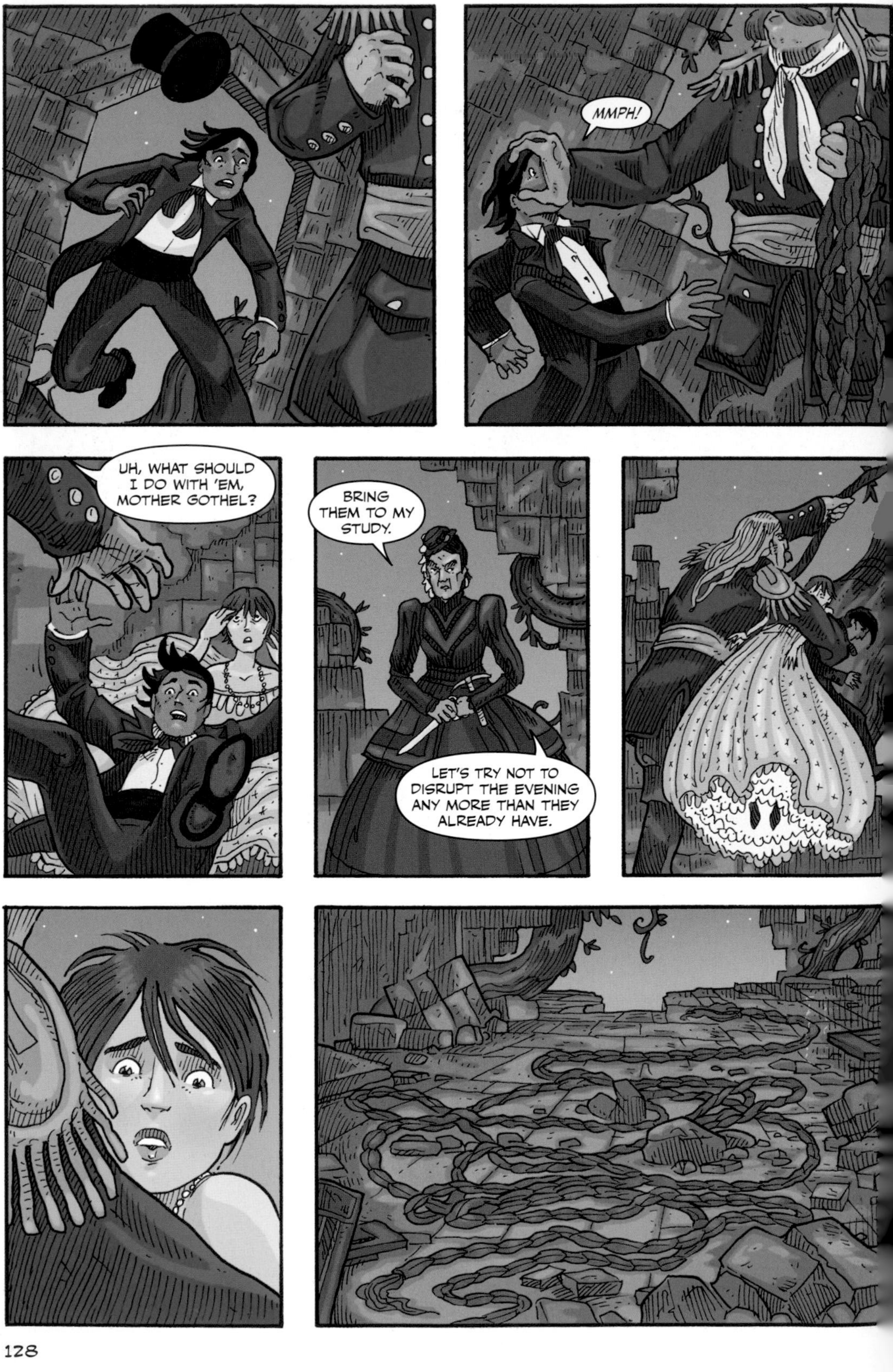
MMPH!
UH, WHAT SHOULD I DO WITH 'EM, MOTHER GOTHEL?
BRING THEM TO MY STUDY.
LET'S TRY NOT TO DISRUPT THE EVENING ANY MORE THAN THEY ALREADY HAVE.

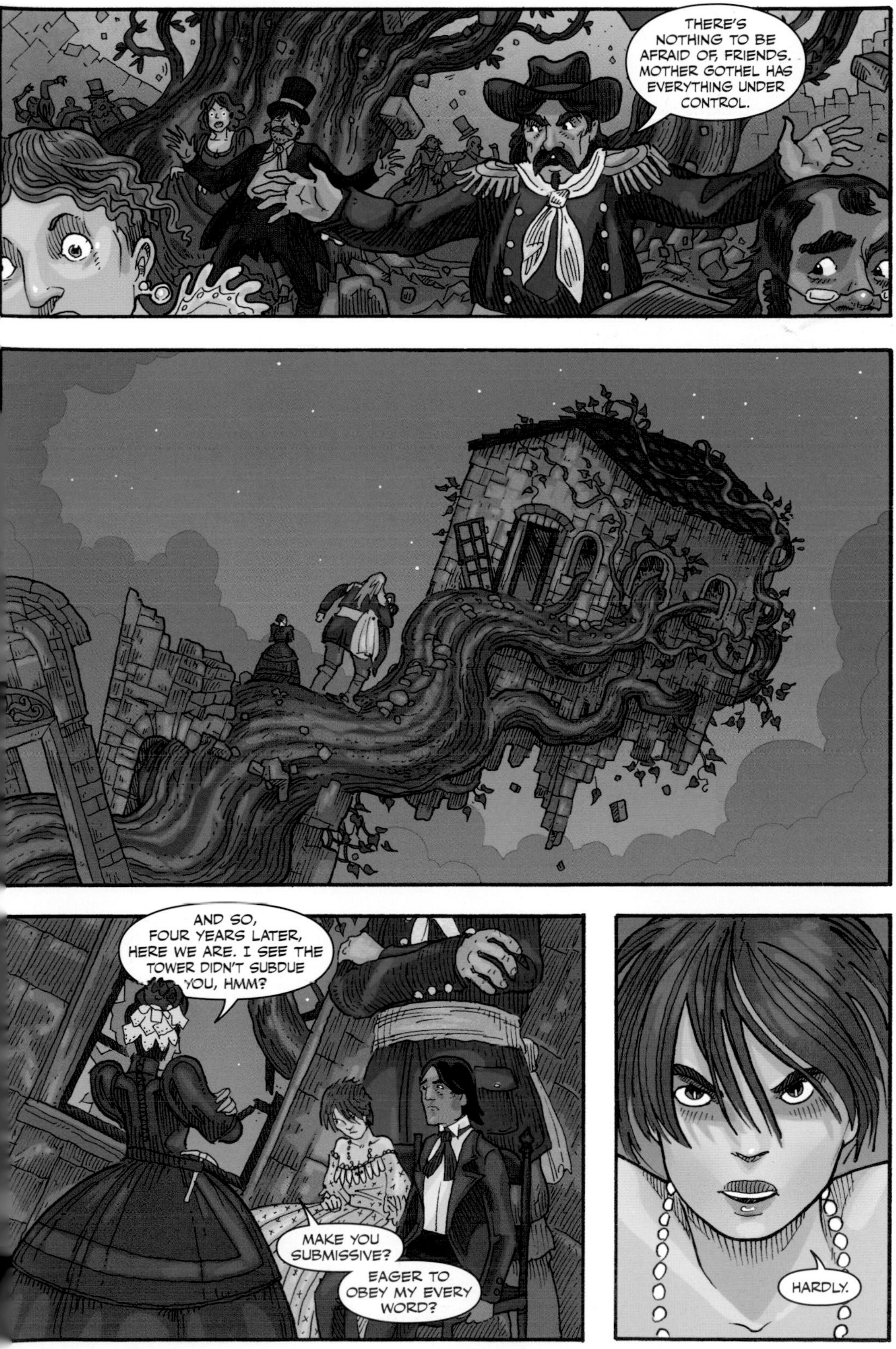
THERE'S NOTHING TO BE AFRAID OF, FRIENDS. MOTHER GOTHEL HAS EVERYTHING UNDER CONTROL.
AND SO, FOUR YEARS LATER, HERE WE ARE. I SEE THE TOWER DIDN'T SUBDUE YOU, HMM?
MAKE YOU SUBMISSIVE?
EAGER TO OBEY MY EVERY WORD?
HARDLY.

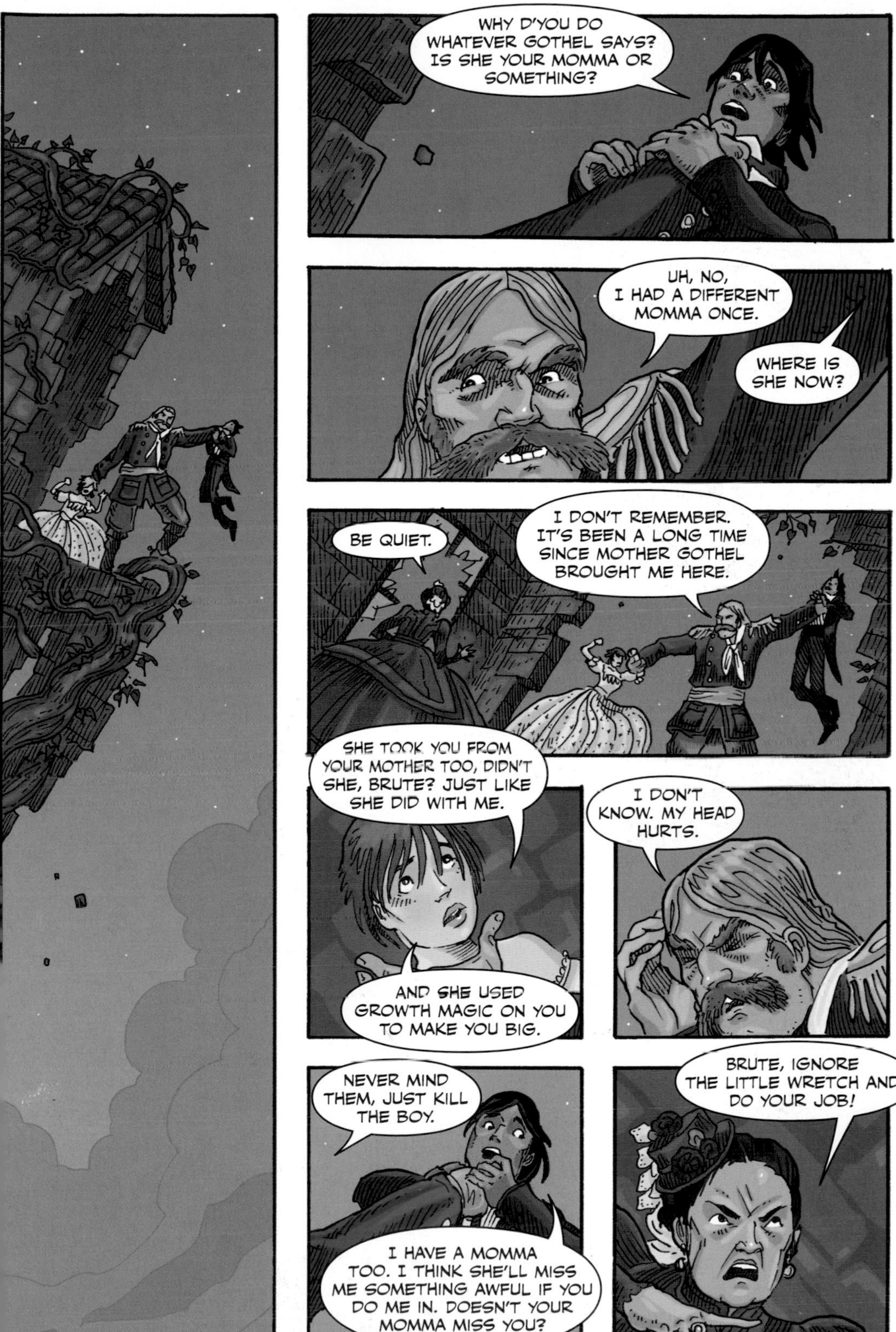
WHY D'YOU DO WHATEVER GOTHEL SAYS? IS SHE YOUR MOMMA OR SOMETHING?
UH, NO, I HAD A DIFFERENT MOMMA ONCE.
WHERE IS SHE NOW?
BE QUIET.
I DON'T REMEMBER. IT'S BEEN A LONG TIME SINCE MOTHER GOTHEL BROUGHT ME HERE.
SHE TOOK YOU FROM YOUR MOTHER TOO, DIDN'T SHE, BRUTE? JUST LIKE SHE DID WITH ME.
AND SHE USED GROWTH MAGIC ON YOU TO MAKE YOU BIG.
I DON'T KNOW. MY HEAD HURTS.
NEVER MIND THEM, JUST KILL THE BOY.
I HAVE A MOMMA TOO. I THINK SHE'LL MISS ME SOMETHING AWFUL IF YOU DO ME IN. DOESN'T YOUR MOMMA MISS YOU?
BRUTE, IGNORE THE LITTLE WRETCH AND DO YOUR JOB!

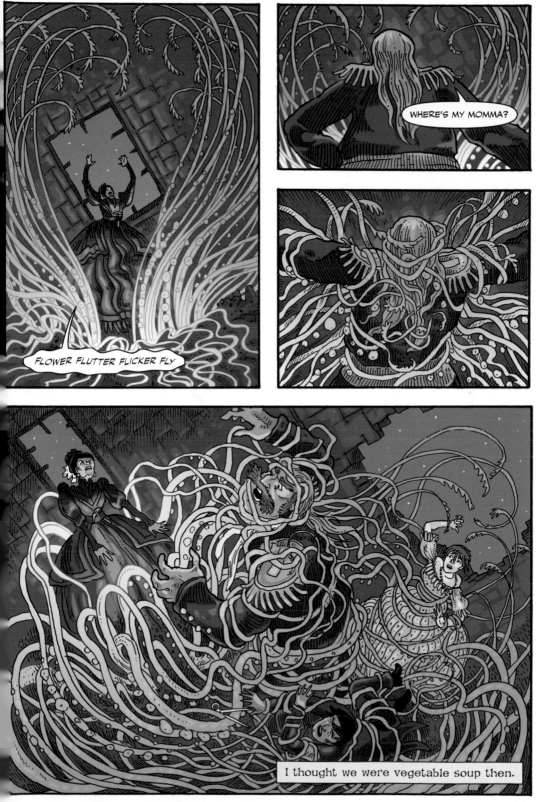

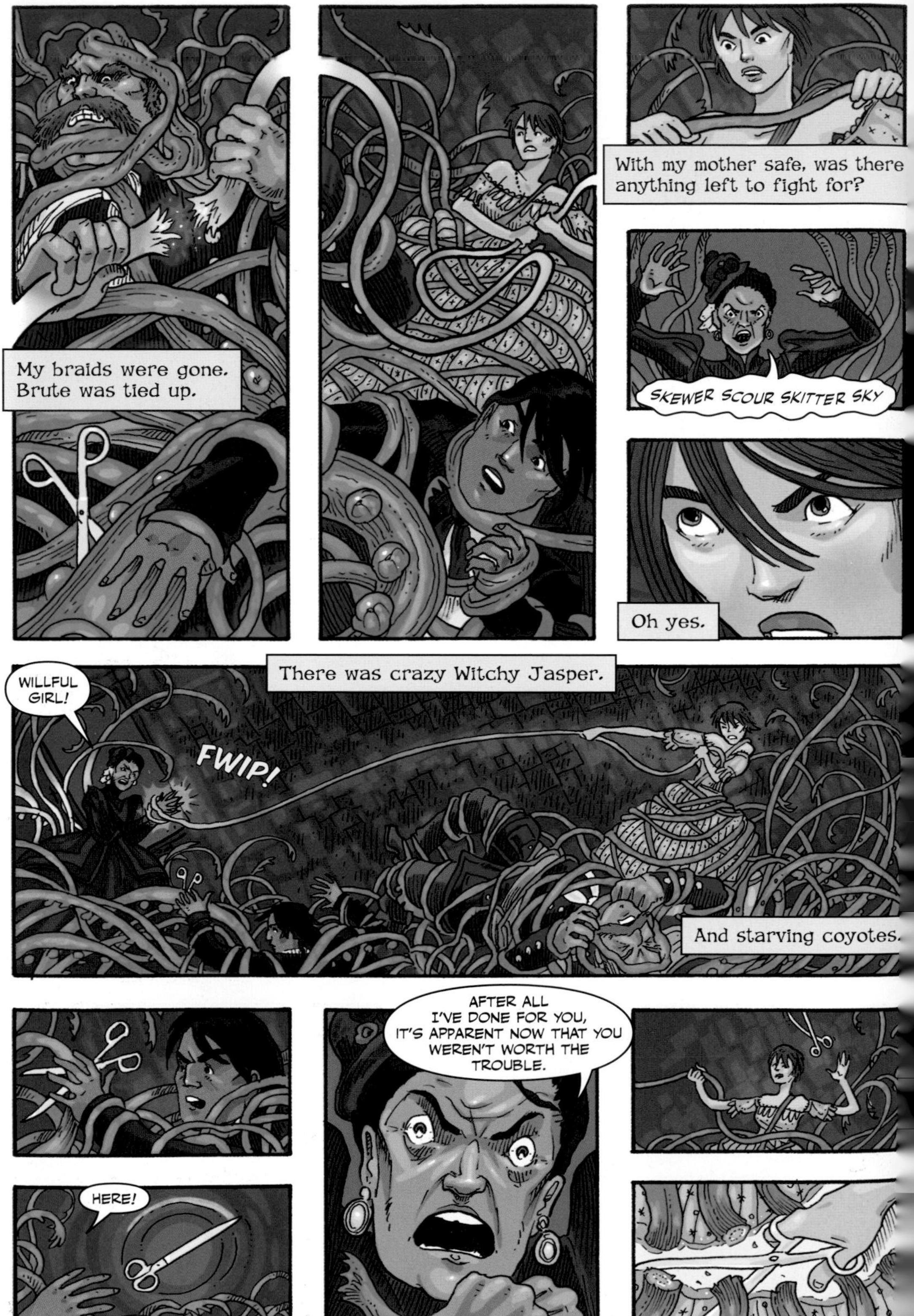

My braids were gone. Brute was tied up.
With my mother safe, was there anything left to fight for?
SKEWER SCOUR SKITTER SKY
Oh yes.
There was crazy Witchy Jasper.
WILLFUL GIRL!
FWIP!
And starving coyotes.
AFTER ALL I'VE DONE FOR YOU, IT'S APPARENT NOW THAT YOU WEREN'T WORTH THE TROUBLE.
HERE!

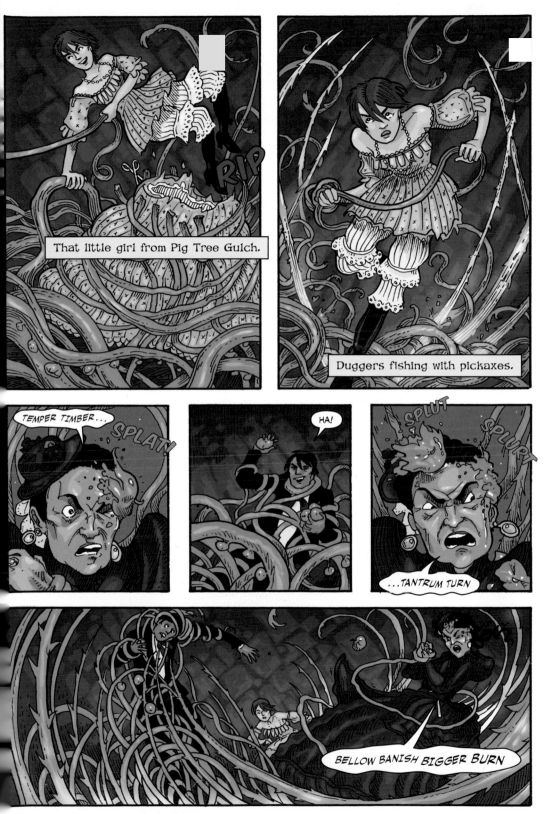

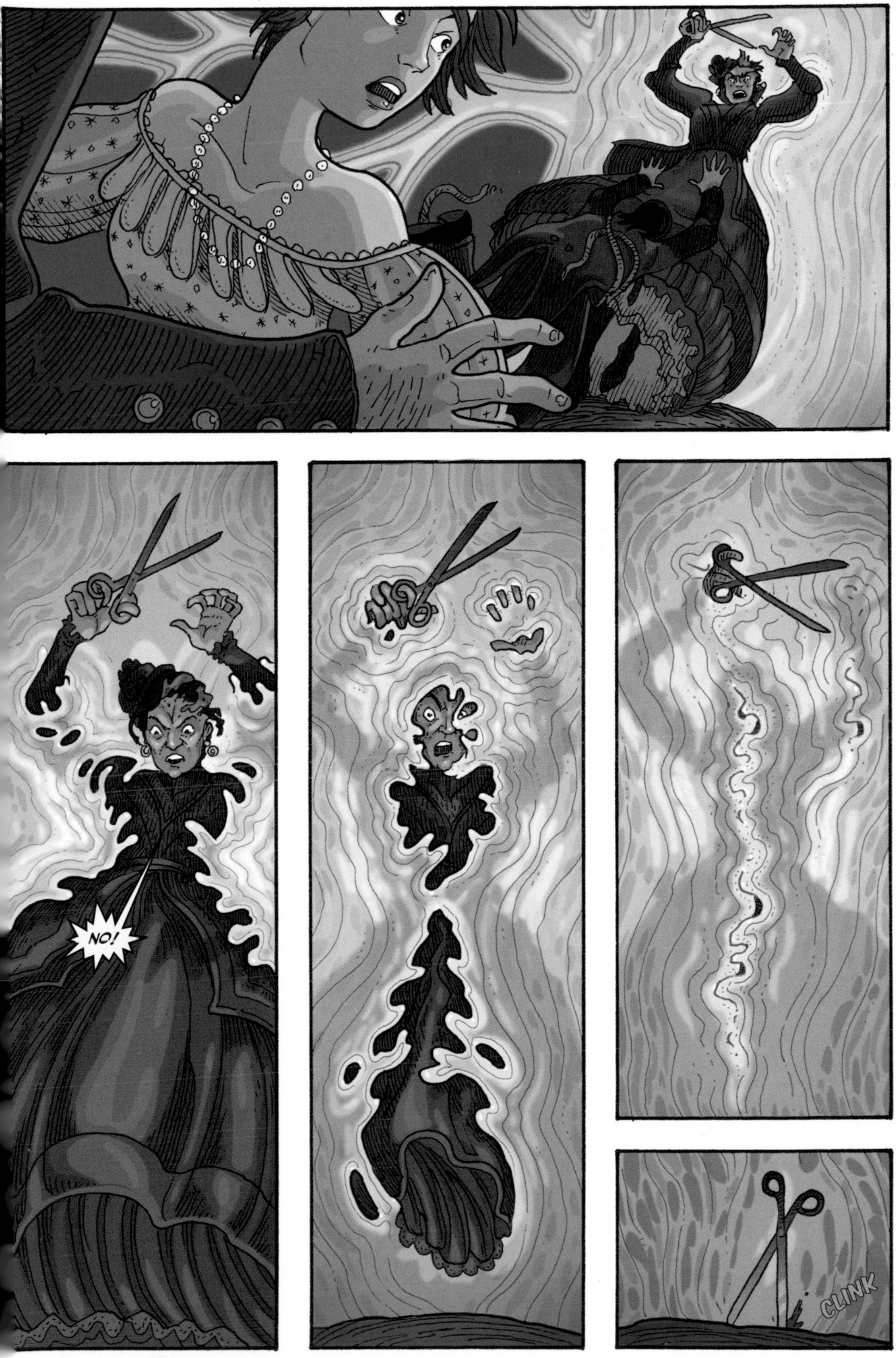
NO!
CLINK

The rest of the night was maybe the busiest and happiest of my life.

YAY!

FREE!

HURRAY!

YEE-HAW!

AT LAST.

There was some cleaning up to do with Gothel's henchmen...

Of course, we couldn't let that nice shindig go to waste.

And everyone from the mines had a midnight house-moving party.

Mostly my momma and I talked. A drink of water in a desert is good, but this was better.

She called me Annie. I like that. But I'm still going to keep the name Rapunzel too. I don't want to forget any part of my story.

Around sunrise, I thought I'd get out and see if the land was changing since Gothel's downfall...

...but the gate was clogged up. So I had to find another way....

PUNZIE? HEY, PUNZIE! LET YOUR HAIR BACK DOWN! I WANT TO CLIMB UP!

JACK, LOOK AT ALL THAT GREEN. I RECKON THAT'S WHAT THIS LAND USED TO LOOK LIKE, BEFORE SHE SUCKED IT DRY.

LACEY'S VILLAGE TOO. DO YOU THINK THE DUGGERS WOULD ACCEPT AN INVITATION TO RETURN TO THE MINES?

MAYBE THOSE COYOTES WILL STAY PUT NOW.

WITHOUT A DOUBT.

LET ME MAKE A WILD GUESS ABOUT WHAT DESTROYED YOUR MOTHER'S HOUSE...

...SOMETHING THAT STARTED WITH "BEAN" AND ENDED WITH "STALK."

THAT PARTICULAR STALK TOOK A LOT LONGER TO GROW. I DIDN'T RECKON HOW FAST THIS ONE WOULD SPROUT IN GOTHEL'S MAGIC GARDEN.

NOT TO GET ALL NAMBY-PAMBY, BUT THANKS FOR HELPING ME.

IT WAS ENTIRELY MY PLEASURE.

UH...WELL, I GUESS IT'S ABOUT TIME WE RETURNED THOSE HORSES. DO YOU THINK BEARDED HENRY WOULD LET ME BUY THEM?

I'VE GOTTEN PRETTY ATTACHE TO MINE. I NAME HIM ROGER.

142

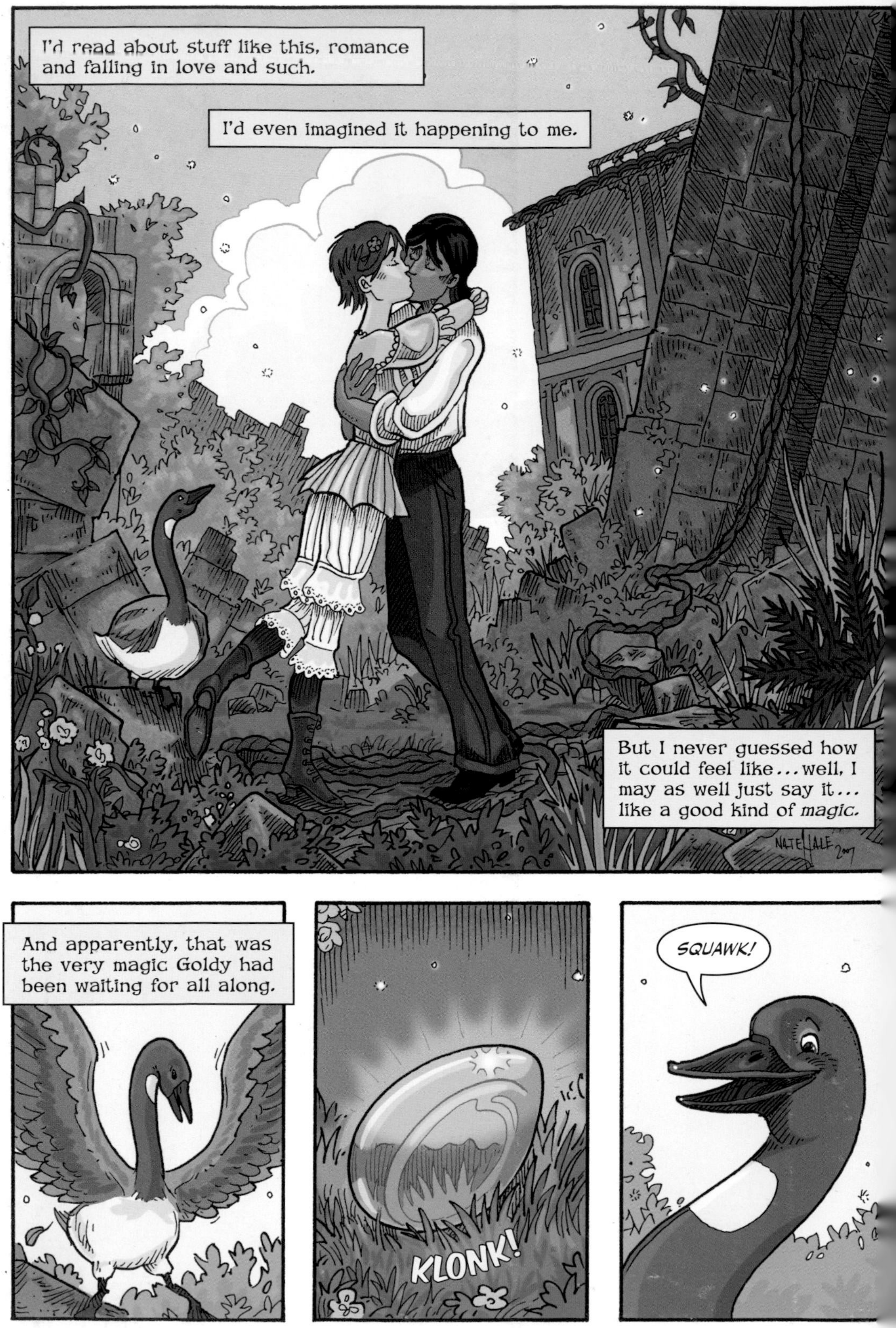
I'd read about stuff like this, romance and falling in love and such.
I'd even imagined it happening to me.
But I never guessed how it could feel like... well, I may as well just say it... like a good kind of *magic.*
NATE HALE 2007
And apparently, that was the very magic Goldy had been waiting for all along.
KLONK!
SQUAWK!